TALES FROM THE INNER CITY

TALES FROM T

SHAUN TAN

HE INNER CITY

WALKER STUDIO
AN IMPRINT OF WALKER BOOKS

The animals of the world exist
for their own reasons.

Alice Walker

Crocodiles live on the eighty-seventh floor. And very comfortably, too. Plenty of filtered water, mud, swamp grass, climate control, fresh meat delivered twice a week, big long walls of uninterrupted glass along which to follow the sun all day, slowly moving from east to west; such luxurious reptilian basking would never be possible at ground level. Did I mention the spectacular view of the financial district in all directions? The wetland recordings ducted in through hidden vents, like an eternal loop of nature's original muzak? What I mean to say is that these animals live in timeless peace. Every day is the same day, months go by without name or number and the years evaporate high above the rushing, grinding, tidal heat of traffic we poor saps have to deal with.

Do the crocodiles even know where they are, you ask? More to the point, how is it that the workers who fill the rest of the building never consider that the word *crocodiles* next to that single lift button is anything more than an abstraction – fashion label? insurance? advertising? high tech? – surely one of a several thousand firms in this city with whom they have no account, no appointment, and to whom they owe no attention. Nothing shrinks the imagination like a waiting room, and a lift is nothing if not the smallest of all waiting rooms.

Workers on the floor below once noticed a leaky ceiling, but that was fixed decades ago. Workers on the floor above would never believe the writhing mass of prehistoric lizard just below their patent-leather shoes. Yet this they do know: fall asleep at your desk and you'll be running naked through a dark forest screaming terrified monkey gibberish, only to wake with a rush of overwhelming exhilaration and clarity, of feeling absolutely alive. Since they introduced office hammocks the business success of floor eighty-eight has become legendary. They call it inspiration, as hairless apes will do. Crocodiles know better.

No, the only people who actually know about eighty-seven are a handful of building inspectors, city planners and maintenance guys like me, and we generally keep it to ourselves. Not that it's any big secret. Just that whenever I tell people crocodiles are up there, they either think I'm crazy or stand there dumb, waiting for a punchline about lawyers that never arrives. Convince them of the simple, physical fact and their disbelief quickly sours into judgement: it's against nature, it's inhumane, it's creepy and cruel and weird and wrong, they should all be returned to their natural habitat! And so forth. I just shrug and get on with my job. Debate makes me weary, and I get no pleasure from the irony any more.

I mean, nobody even remembers that this whole city was built on a swamp. The crocodiles, well, they've been living in this very spot for a million years and I'll bet they'll still be here long after the traffic has ground itself back into mud and we hairless apes conclude our final meeting, declare bankruptcy and move on, as hairless apes will do. In the cool brain of a crocodile the city is just a waiting room: the biggest of all waiting rooms, rising up through an age with which they have no account, no appointment, and to which they owe no attention.

The butterflies came at lunchtime. Not millions, billions or even trillions but a number beyond counting, beyond even the *concept* of counting, so that people on the street were relieved of any estimation. By people on the street, I mean everyone. Literally *everyone*. No earthquake, fire or terrorist attack could flush so many out of cars, apartments, subways, restaurants, hotels, stores, banks, hospitals, schools, parliaments and offices. None had ever experienced such inexplicable, joyful urgency.

And as if in response, the butterflies came to us, descending from dizzying heights like spring blossoms of every imaginable colour and pattern. Gliding, skipping, fluttering around our ears in soundless wonder. We were standing so still, shoulder to shoulder, stalled as traffic on bridges, every breath held and every eye open, waiting for the weightless blessing of tiny insects. *Look! Look! There on your shoulder, your arm, your knee, your head! Hold still! Don't move! Look at this one right here on my nose!* And for that briefest of moments, faces and palms to the sky, we did not ask why. The chatter in our heads fell silent, the endless ticker tape of voice-over narrative, always prying things apart for cause and effect, sign and symbol, some kind of useful meaning or value or portent – it all just stopped, and the butterflies came to us.

Later they would leave, technicolour clouds billowing up and drifting away to the west. Later our minds would quickly snap back to factory settings and the chatter would resume. Was this an omen of something good or bad? A plague? A system out of whack? A divine message? A lesson in chaos? What did it mean? *What did it mean?* Later we would study photo and video evidence with furrowed brows, listen to media analysis, consult scripture and meteorology, look at maps, graphs, stats and bell curves. Later we would worry.

But for now, for that briefest of all moments, we did not ask why. We thought of nothing but the butterflies, the butterflies settling on our heads, on the heads of friends and family, on everyone we knew and everyone we didn't, on the whole city all at once. *Don't move,* we whispered, wishing it could last for ever. *Hold still! Hold still! Hold still!*

Once we were strangers,
legs bent the wrong way,
rough voices falling to the wind,
every tooth and claw and stick a weapon,
every urge a ragged mystery.

But we always wanted more than this.
In our hearts we knew there was more.

One day I threw my stick at you.
You brought it back.
My hand touched your ear.
Your nose touched the back of my knee.
Then we were walking side by side
as if it had always been this way.

Time flowed out before us,
an endless river,
the plains opened up, the sky lifted,
and you cried out to me then:
This world is ours!
And so it was.

When I ran, you ran.
When you called, I answered.
Together we chased away all loneliness and fear,
and saw everything happen that was ever going to happen,
every beauty and terror, every rise and fall.

And when you died
I took you down to the river.
And when I died
you waited for me by the shore.
So it was that time passed between us.

And then, somehow, we were together again.
This is how it's always been.

But now everything is different.
The river flows wrongly,
the plains are gone,
the sky presses down like a thousand ceilings.
It feels like time is only ever running away from us.
Where will we go? What will we do?

You pull at my hand,
push your nose into the back of my knee,
and cry out to me as you always do,
This world is ours!
And just like that
we are walking again.

The public called them indecent. Politicians called them unacceptable. Religious leaders called them unholy. Even naturalists called them unnatural. They came anyway, like a cool breeze that blows through a hot and restless night, those gigantic snails, finding each other in the byways and intersections of our great city and making love right then and there, answering every shout of indignation with grace and pride and the slowest of slow dances in the dark. One hundred years on and who can remember what all the fuss was about? Who can now imagine our city without these beautiful creatures? We would be so sad if they ever went away, leaving us all alone with our small ideas about love.

The monster of our nightmares was finally dead, dragged from the harbour after years of struggle. Cables, ropes, hooks and winches: the city had used everything at its disposal, every drop of diesel, sweat and cunning. The maw – and that was the strange word that hung in our minds like strands of bloody mucous – was bigger than a house, bigger than an office block, and surely this was a thing that would swallow entire communities without a blink of its dead black eye, and still be hungry. That much we knew. That much we almost certainly knew. And yet here it was, defeated by the people it had once terrorized. We had killed it. We had won.

Thousands turned out for the cutting, and oh how we cheered. For once in this godforsaken town the stench of death was sweet. It drifted up along the canyons of industry and piqued some appetite deep within us, some thirst. Everybody wanted to look into that maw. That cavernous maw. All those teeth. They could no longer hurt us. And the huge hooks that yanked at the beast's nose, pulling it high into a spine-breaking arch, contorting every streamlined grace with grinding gears ... well, none could wish for a more fitting indignity.

The Fisherman clambered along the truck bed with his massive hockey-stick flensing knife and we cheered anew. He seemed weary beyond purpose, our hero of the day, his overalls slicked with oil and blood and brine, his movements slack and joyless, as if the city had not already paid him a king's ransom. His beard hung like a curtain and we couldn't hear what he said when he took the medal from the mayor and put it in his pocket, instead of wearing it around his neck. He didn't look at us when we sang the song. All this we happily forgave. We waited for his blade to bite the gut of the monster, a sickly white belly that had never been touched by the sun, a horribly smooth mass the colour of spoiled milk: what treasures or horrors would it divulge? The mayor searched for a word that meant both disgust and delight, but couldn't find one. It didn't matter. With a sudden grunt, the Fisherman leaned all his weight into the knife, broke into a run, and the monster unzipped.

The roar of the crowd suddenly changed in pitch: it morphed into a low animal sound, a long moan that came from deep beneath the lungs. We heard it before we even knew we were the ones making it: *MWOOOAAAR!* And like a sack of slurry dumped onto a street, that moan flattened out into gasps and gags, then a smattering of laughs that had nothing to do with laughing, but rather the collapse of all civilized language. The sight and smell hit us like a wave. Our stomachs inverted. We couldn't back off fast enough, slipping and stumbling. And there, through the membranous muck, a sense of something thrashing, lots of things thrashing.

The Fisherman did not hesitate. He picked up a slightly smaller flensing knife, and strode through the stringy fluid to cut open all the new ones. Mouths like crystal necklaces gasping for a sea they would never know as the life drained out of them; and from their own pale bellies rolled even more sharks, smaller ones, each thrashing hopefully. The Fisherman took another knife from his belt, a single-hander now, and on he went.

We turned away before the butchering came to an end, assuming that it did, in fact, come to an end. The sharks just kept spilling out like Russian dolls, smaller and smaller, hundreds, thousands, each unborn generation as fresh and blue as water before they rolled out into the blood and gore of their parents, grandparents, great-grandparents... the last we saw were no bigger than a finger.

We searched for words that didn't exist, wondered why we needed them so badly, then went home. The Fisherman didn't look at any of us, not once, just kept on cutting, even after they turned off the floodlights.

She noticed the first poster taped roughly to the launderette window: *LOST: grey and white cat, no collar, answers to the name Captain Plush, reward*. The second was outside the supermarket: *Macbeth is MISSING! Extremely friendly, much loved family member.* Another at the day care centre two blocks away: *Have you seen our Jonah? Missing since Tuesday. Please help!* Then at the welfare office: *LOST CAT. Very big one. Name Ling Ling.*

And so on: *Catnip, Haniko, Bean-Bag, Amadeus, Potato King, Sanjeev, Earl Grey, Mustafa.*

So many lost cats, where had they all gone? She soon stopped looking, especially at all those badly cropped, grainy, underexposed pictures. It was all too upsetting given what had just happened to her own cat. Poor Tugboat. He had been watching TV with them, as he did religiously for an hour every evening before bolting away to some urgent business at the other end of their fire escape. Except for that one time, two weeks ago, when he'd slunk in slow and listless, curled up on the couch and stayed in that same spot. By morning he was cold and stiff. The stark reality of it was inconceivable. It was as if Tugboat had just crept away in the night and left this effigy behind, a taxidermied imposter, a heavy and graceless lump of some other cat on their couch.

It was devastating for many reasons, not least because Tugboat happened to be, by every assessment of her young daughter, the greatest cat in the world. In the absence of real friends the little girl loved the animal like a brother. She now cried at breakfast and cried at dinner, and then at every picture of a cat, especially if it was a striped one. Even so, as they strolled hand in hand past yet another lost cat poster, her daughter took a break between sobs to look very closely and observe the most obvious and unsentimental of facts, one that had somehow eluded her mother.

"Now we know where Tugboat went when he wasn't at home," she said, blowing her nose unceremoniously. "And why he was so fat."

And yes, there it was – the same small cut on every ear, the same odd tooth, and that evasive look he always gave a camera. The two of them had buried Tugboat, wrapped in his special blanket, in the only patch of dirt available in their concrete blight of a courtyard, sufficiently godforsaken to allow them to dig a hole with a kitchen ladle. As they stood side by side reading crayoned eulogies, placing trinkets on the mound – his favourite ball, his mouse, his silver bowl – both of them knew something was slightly amiss. Again, it was just an effigy they were burying, not the actual cat. The mother found it frustratingly difficult to weep. She dabbed her eyes anyway and studied her daughter's uneven braids as the girl bent down to rearrange the flowers one more time.

She couldn't even remember the last time she wept. Certainly it was long before they moved to this charmless ghetto of strange faces, broken fixtures and unclassifiable smells and stains to begin their "new life" (God, how she loathed that phrase). Once upon a time tears ran like a river through her body, always a merciful relief, but that was the past. Now everything just emptied into a black sea, with one dark wave rising after another; each angry, foaming lip threatened to peak and break and crash, only to subside at the last moment, making room for yet another swell, another rising line of whiplashed foam, another promise of destruction withheld. Why was it that she wished so much for that surge to just tumble down once and for all? Sinking everything, drowning everything. Was she a terrible mother to think such things? She was just so tired of treading water.

The daughter knew about the waves, in the way that children do. She too saw them rising in the distance as they stood by the grave, but she did not wish for one thing or another. She only thought about Tugboat.

He had bounded through the window one evening, another stray soul looking for a little warmth and a bite to eat, and just accepted things as they were, as if things had always been this way, without interest in the past or the future: for cats such things do not exist. There was only ever the continuous here and now: a patter of sweet meows, a soulful green stare, a furry weight at the end of an exhausting day, a cure for every qualm and misery measured out in purrs. Right from the start it was clear Tugboat wasn't just any cat. He was the tiny vessel shunting them steadfastly through the dark sea, one day at a time. And now he was dead … sort of.

Which was probably why the posters caught her eye in the first place, the mother realized, things she normally would never bother to read, having no need for more crappy furniture or the misspelt problems of others. Here were pictures of *their* cat, photographed on the sofas of strangers, haunting the scriptless and heel-worn circuits of their day-to-day lives. It had to mean something, and as usual her daughter was the one to say it: "I think Tugboat needs our help."

And so they collected all the information, deciding together what to say on the phone or write in reply: *We're so sorry to inform you that your cat* – insert name here – *died peacefully and has been laid to rest at this address. There will be a small memorial service on Sunday*, and so on. For good measure, they also made their own poster advertising the funeral, in case there were further "owners", but there was the problem of picking the right name for the animal. "The Greatest Cat in The World," said the girl, so that's what they wrote under the photo, and then they went out to post copies everywhere.

On Sunday the visitors arrived one after another, following glitter-glue arrows to the building courtyard. At first a few, then a dozen, and then even more, coming in from all directions, too many to count.

Each mourner left small objects on the grave, until it was not so much a grave as a shrine: bowls and toys – each one a singular favourite – ringed by flowers, photos and drawings. There were odd little parcels of food, incense, peculiar gestures and what might have been prayers. The faces of all the men, women and children were both strange and familiar. How many times had they passed each other silently, if not warily – you might even say catlike – at the supermarket, the launderette, doctors' waiting rooms, their very own apartment stairs? Some spoke their same language and some didn't – the cat clearly had a broad taste for multicultural cuisine – but none of that mattered because they all knew the animal by every name imaginable, they all knew what a wonderful friend he was and how sorry they were that he was no more.

The talking, the sighing, the laughing and sobbing, all of it merged together like the sound of black water crashing around the mother's ears, not loud and booming as she always expected such annihilation to be, but soft, like a splay of foam dissolving into a sandy shore, and finally she wept. Her daughter looked up. "It's the sound of Tugboat coming down off the couch and going up the fire escape," she said. And just like that the greatest cat in the world was gone.

You are two years old. You are in a car being driven home from the city. Your parents loom silently before you, stoic and reassuring like mountains in the night. Father: big hands on the wheel, the glow of the dash, green and red and white. Mother: saying something, tiny treasures sparkling on her earlobes. Panes of light and shadow, orange, brown, this one yellow or grey, running over your knees and up the back of the seat in front of you, growing, fading, regenerating, as the streetlamps gallop through your backseat world.

"Horses," you shout suddenly, "look at the horses!"

Mother asks: "What horses?"

"Up there!"

Father says: "No horses in the city, pumpkin."

But you look and see them there as plain as day. Horses running along fast lanes, rooftops and flyovers, even along the jib of cranes and electrical wires strung high in the air. In a moment they are right alongside the car, close enough for you to see their rolling marble eyes and wind-rippled manes and hear the pounding rush of their breath against the window.

Run with us a while, they say, *and we'll tell you a story.*

You take it in as only a two-year-old can, like any other story about tigers or elephants or rainbows or unicorns, all things being equal in stories. This one is about horses, horses that carry a whole city on their backs. There it is, rising up through the heat and dust, brick by brick, barrel by barrel, in some long-ago dreamtime when blood came before diesel and the streets reeked of manure, and the incessant din of clip-clopping hooves left every crack of the whip deaf to clemency. Horses pulling freight and people, the dirt of massive urban excavation, huge dead-axle drays carting ice, iron, meat, beer and coal, and all the things that make a city run. Crowded omnibuses shunting human bodies back and forth long before trams or automobiles were even thought about. Horses grinding metal shoes against cobblestones, pulling loads beyond all natural measure up endless hills and corridors of heat and snow. Horses walking round and round driving nothing but millstones and conveyor belts and crank shafts with shuttered eyes and ears struck numb by the blast of factory whistles. Horses bought and sold, groomed and beaten, working to sleep and sleeping to work, and fires lit under their bellies when they fail to rouse in the quiet hours before any other creature is expected to stir. Carved in the timbers of multi-storey stables, the mantra of their keepers: *sentiment pays no dividend*. Horses know this more than most: the greatest curse of any animal is to be worth money to men.

The city grows and grows. Now it's so packed with horses that they crash about like cars, eventually falling down, being towed away and piled into a flyblown heap in factory back lots. The city demands no requiem for the faithful, only further coin from a knackered corpse: stripped down for dog meat and candle fat, bones burnt and ground down into fertilizer, skins tooled into straps and fastened to the withers of their offspring, ligaments boiled for furniture glue and, like some terrible belated retribution, a blight of fly-borne typhoid rising up from vast pits of manure that nobody knows what to do with.

Only the souls of horses are, mercifully, of no use to men, not worth a dollar. They shake themselves loose. They dream of running along some green and grassy ancestral plain. They'll never find it.

But run they must, and so they run through the city, as far as they can go, night after night. They tell you all this in a wordless language of heaving sighs; they look down at you without malice or sadness or regret, only dispassionate equine curiosity. Wondering why things are the way they are, understanding no more of the world than a toddler passing by in some other century.

Now they've stopped, having run all the way to the city limits, the world beyond too strange entirely, a place they were never born to know. They stand together in the cool dark, nodding and braying, restlessly stamping their hooves on concrete as you speed away. *Remember us,* they whinny, *remember us, remember us!*

But you won't remember; you are only two years old.

Later you'll come to love horses with a depth you can't explain and many horses will love you back. Sometimes in this faraway universe your eyes will skip to the wires loping along the motorway as you drive home from the stables and you'll be struck by the notion that what flows there is something darker than electricity, that the shadow along the flyover is something more than a shadow. But here in the past, two years old, there are no questions. You can still see them all clearly enough, all those city horses standing and stamping, even as they slip from the rear-view mirror and are released back into the night.

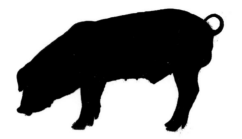

In the room at the back of our apartment there
is a pig, sinking. Or maybe sinking isn't the right word. What I mean is
that it's disappearing, bit by bit, piece by piece – or rather, slice by slice.
And because the vanishing slices are those resting on the concrete floor,
it looks just like sinking, only very slowly, so slowly you hardly notice. If
the pig lifted up what once were its trotters, you would see nothing there.
Nothing in the concrete, nothing on the pig, not even a stump … it's kind
of hard to explain. Why are they even called trotters anyway? It's not like
the pig can trot anywhere. It just stays in the room at the back of our
apartment, just like every other pig in every other family in every other
city apartment, sinking. One day it will be completely gone, and we'll have
to get another pig. Then it will happen all over again.

Does it hurt? Does it make the pig sad? Dad says no, and he must
be right, because the pig doesn't cry or make much noise. But maybe pigs
suffer in a way we can't know. Who can say for sure what another animal
is feeling? Dad tells us to stop looking at the pig if it bothers us so much:

just keep the door closed and don't forget to turn out the light. But then we can't help thinking about the pig even more, all alone in the dark, getting less and less. Maybe it wants to go out sometimes, meet other pigs, trot around or whatever it can do with what's left. Maybe the pig has a family, just like us. What if it has brothers and sisters? Wouldn't it want to visit them? Dad says no, it does not have or would not want anything like that. But he says it in a funny way that leaves us thinking that maybe Dad doesn't know everything, and we see that he sees that we are thinking this, and we know that he knows that we know, and he says, "Look, I don't like it any more than you do." Then he gives a big sigh the way he does. We turn out the light and join Mum at the dinner table.

Later, when everyone is asleep, when every clock stops in the gap between yesterday and tomorrow and the world turns blue, we sneak out. We take the pig. This is something we are not allowed to do. But we have made a special trolley from oven trays and roller skates anyway. The pig is excited. We can tell this from the bit of waggly tail that's left: it's waggling like crazy. The streets are blue, the cars are blue, the empty shops, the empty avenues, bluer than blue, and so are we and so is the pig and the moon is huge. We roll him all the way to the park and screw on the trotters we made out of cardboard tubes and paint. Look at him go! Flying like a rocket down the path, over the grass and into the moonlit field where all the other pigs are milling about. Listen to them all grunting and squealing, meeting their brothers and sisters and telling each other everything they know and everything they don't. What a ruckus! If you hold your hands up just above your eyes, the buildings and wires and streetlights disappear, so that all you can see are trees and pigs. Then you can imagine it's always been like this. Just trees and pigs in the moonlight, for ever and ever.

Consider this: there's no ocean in our city. No lake, and no river. Well no real river, more like a chemical drain that runs upside down with all the muck on top, and maybe dead things too, if there is anything left to die in all that blackness, somewhere beneath the motorway where all forgotten things go. Pumps beneath the city work night and day and have done for centuries, keeping the subways dry. The only place left for a fish here, the only untouched openness with any tide or current, well, it's the sky. So that's what you have to get near to if you want to catch a fish, and half the trouble of urban fishing is getting to the top of the tallest building you can find without anyone noticing. Especially with gear. Lines, tackle, buckets and big black balloons filled with helium, which of course aren't so cheap, going up as they do and rarely coming back, unless popped by blowies or snarks. You do get funny looks – a bunch of kids climbing stairwells at midnight, all decked out in black, with rods and balloons – but we are used to funny looks.

OK, so assuming you find a good and accessible spot, that nobody else either knows about or has any prior claim to, chances are you're settling in for a very long and dull time. The air might be moving the wrong way, the night the wrong night, the season the wrong season, the moon in the wrong phase, or you're using the wrong bait or line altitude or whatnot: everyone has their own half-baked theory. It's all bunk. Nobody knows fish but fish. Even if you can see their faint shapes against all the light pollution that hides them so well, even if you spot the flickering lights as their iridescent eyes catch the reflections of stadiums, shopping and red light districts, and even if you get your balloon-lofted hook close to where their mouths must be, they almost never bite, just brush past like slow-wandering nothings. They are just not interested in earthly things, and who can blame them? But you must also know this: people who fish in dry cities are not normal people, just as the fish are not normal fish, and so we are used to sitting around in the dark doing nothing but feeling the vibration of switching winds on a dumb thread poised against our fingers, for hours on end, until our arses feel like pincushions, our stomachs growl and our eyelids call it quits. Call it stupidity or fun.

We do catch things sometimes, of course, us kids being better at it than oldies, but the truth is that in all our years of doing this we only ever caught gobblers and snarks: small, grey and flat, like a deflated balloon full of bones, only good for cats. One or two a night, if anything, just to keep Pushkin happy. But there was always the great and ridiculous dream of every urban sky angler, snagging a big one: a golden stratus, a wahoo, a strafe, a neon mulloway, a brownstone dollarfish or pretty much any kind of blackfin celestial. Moonfish? A dream beyond dreams. People talked about it, told stories of near things and luckless sightings, but never furnished by a gram of proof. So when I caught it, when we caught it – when Pim caught it, I mean – you can imagine the shock. Not least because Pim never catches anything, not even gobblers and snarks.

I watched him sometimes, always ready to chastise him for wasting balloons and bait. He did everything right except fish: he cut up the kitchen scraps and mixed burley with fishy oil poured off the top of sardine cans, and sent the line up OK, but I never saw him jerk. "Any bites?" I'd ask, and he'd nod, and sure enough reel down the hook nibbled shiny bare. "You gotta jerk on it, dammit. They're not going to catch themselves!" He'd say, "I know, I know" and then go on like that, sitting like a rock, not moving his hand an inch, and sometimes holding the line between his teeth so he could "hear what the fish were doing", which of course made a good elbow jerk nigh impossible. He was the smallest of all of us and I let it go. He caught nothing but loved it anyway: like I said, stupidity or fun.

But that one hot night I looked over and saw Pim suddenly stand up black against the boiling city lights and yank his tiny arms all the way down as if bowing to a king or ringing a church bell, only quickly. And he said, "I got it" – not "I got one", which is what you say when you catch a fish, but "I got *it*" – as if this had been the one and only fish he had ever wanted to land, or was ever going to bother trying to land. We all saw the nylon that traced up in to the black night fall loopy, and thought, *here we go, another balloon lost and Pim just being Pim.* But then it zipped back up again, snapping tight like the string on a guitar, with an actual noise we all heard: *twang!* It arced this way and that, some massive invisible pendulum on the end trying to loose itself free. We all rushed to his aid: Jo, Em, Lee and me. "Reel!" we shouted, "Reel, ya numbnut!" Why did he always have to use a hand-line instead of a rod like the rest of us? Like pulling in a kite or winding up yarn for your grandma – no leverage or torque, and painfully slow. He was going to lose it for sure. Or so we thought.

Anyway, what really sent our hearts to gag in our throats was not the catch, it was Pim lifted a clear three metres from the air conditioning duct he had been standing on, and drifting leeward, well, worse than that, streetward. "Oh shit," we yelped, suddenly regretting the whole business. Why on earth did none of us ever remember to clip our tether? Maybe because nobody ever expected to catch anything bigger than their hand, or that a kid might actually weigh less than a floater. To his credit, Pim hung on when the instinct of self-preservation would dictate otherwise, and on a fortuitous downswing wrapped his legs around a chimney pipe like a crazed monkey. Soon the rest of us were on him, grabbing his ankles as if there was no tomorrow – which there almost wasn't given how the tin chimney buckled perilously over the drop – drawing him back from the brink, literally by the bootstraps. And with the big night-fish doing its slow thrash somewhere high and deep, I got a hold of the line to pull hand over fist, taking the force while Pim spooled the slack, steely now, like some yogic algorithm he was born to. This whole time his eyes never once left the sky.

And then we all saw it: in panic the fish must have banked onto its side, turning from an invisible slice of darkness into a great round mirror tilted level to face the city, and we all went quiet. It sparkled like a disc of gold, flash, flash, flash, as it swept around us in a wide circle, trying to find whatever channel of air that might corkscrew it all the way back into the blackness, away from the two things that were surely going to kill it dead: gravity and us. It was the most beautiful thing in the world, that living shape of light drawing its last gyre above our heads.

We were all readying ourselves now, either grabbing the line or each other, fairly certain it would break as it raked low and snagged on rooftop junk, knocking down more than one aerial, which would no doubt attract some corporate strife, but that was the least of our concerns. Even then we suspected our luck to be spent, that we'd never get a chance like this again, ever, and to lose this fish would be a regret beyond regret, and a tale that none would believe without great pangs of doubt: that thought like a strange and anxious sorrow. It's funny how moments of joy can be so tainted. Lee was even running around whacking down aerials with the long gaff with reckless abandon, clearing a space for the line as it swooped lower and lower, snapping off whatever he could, and after a few screaming near misses (us screaming at him to put his back into it), he could just reach out far enough to sink the hooked end of that pole somewhere near the tail, and then we were all pulling on that too. "I told you we needed a gaff!" he beamed, in answer to my constant objections about unnecessary and dangerous angling weaponry. He loved nothing more than proving me wrong.

A stream of something like blood or sparks sprayed out of the wound opening down one side, and we felt the big rhythm of the moonfish's convulsions, that slab of rebellious muscle kicking all the way down our hips and heels as we yanked on line and gaff. It was weakening now, the air down here too heavy and hot, and as it suffocated in that thickness we could see the buoyancy leaving its heavenly body, its swim bladder crushed with a pitiful sigh, and the weight of fatigue pulling it down, finally, finally, to the grey concrete rooftop like a windless kite. We were all over it, piling on, even when gravity was already doing the work, too scared to take chances. It shuddered and gawped and settled in to die. We had caught a moonfish. We had caught a moonfish.

Holy shit, we all thought at once without even needing to say a word, *what will Mum and Dad say about this!* We got it down from the roof fast and quiet before anyone came to inspect what all the whooping noise and busted aerials were about, our veins alight with joyous adrenaline, our faces hot, our accountability zero. We tried not to look at that big lidless eye, once swivelling wildly, now clouding over so fast. It was somehow accusatory in a way we wouldn't properly understand until much later.

The march home through our neighbourhood was the first great gift of the moonfish. Everyone ogled us as we lofted it high, our hands shoved up under the gills, willing to endure the creepy prickles of whatever stratospheric organs it had up there tingling all over our fingers like a thousand dying nerves. Our shirts were sparkly with scales that fell away from the creature like a trail of glitter, and little kids were running out from apartment blocks in their pyjamas to dab it with their fingers, carefully transferring the precious opal flakes into any container they could find. Up close it smelt not like a fish at all, but rather like the blessed rain that follows a very dry summer. Or maybe like the moon. Like a star. Like money.

And how big were Dad's eyes as we busted through the front door! We were so elevated in noble deed, so far above either modesty or gloating, we announced nothing at all – just waltzed into our apartment as if the whole thing was a grand prank, and Dad well knew it. He had seen a moonfish once when he was a boy, as he'd relayed about a thousand times, but even that tiddler was nothing compared to this one. With barely a beat he bent down before us, elbows to the floor. "At your service, my masters!" he bellowed. Before we could even think of a suitable reply, he was up and clearing the kitchen table of all its accumulated evening junk, just dumping armfuls in the sink and calling out for Mum. We hoiked that fish flat on the top, and marvelled at how none of the table was left to see, that the fins draped over the chair backs too, and the tail went all the way to the floor. Then we were all just laughing.

Now some people might liken this kind of happy shock to a family winning a lottery, grabbing each other's arms and jumping up and down like nutjobs: those people don't know much about fish. Money you can get from any place. Not so a moonfish. We were bouncing around the kitchen on invisible trampolines, making sounds that weren't quite human.

That said, it was money on Dad's mind, and Mum, roused from her sleep by all the chaos in the kitchen, could only concur. Much as she winced at the watery antifreeze plasma leaking all over the floor and the general freakishness of this home invasion, she was immediately ticking over the ways in which we might capitalize on this supreme stroke of luck. "Mr Hiro," she said simply, and we all nodded solemnly. "Let's get it ready for Mr Hiro."

How much do I love our family? This much. When any kind of emergency strikes, good or bad, we snap together like parts in a machine, like a submarine crew at war in the tin-can clutter of our home, none of the usual debate, character assassination, woeful monologues and turgid hand-wringing. I've learned to love crises for this reason, how they make us pull together and forget all our separateness and sadness; this was the second great gift of the moonfish. Jo sharpened the knives, Em ran to get ice from downstairs, Pim held the torch, Dad made the incisions, and Lee mopped his brow with a tea towel rolled up between barbecue tongs – a bona fide surgeon's assistant, despite the absence of sweat. Mum prudently pointed out the "dead man's fingers" behind the intestines that needed cutting before they ruptured so close to sea-level and tainted the pearlescent flesh around them, not unlike defusing a bomb, and mentioned a good many other things that saved our bacon, or rather our moonfish fillets. How she knew all this was a mystery, but that in and of itself was nothing new: "I lived many lives before you all came along," she was so fond of saying in a smug way that, for once, we did not find annoying. And thusly instructed, Dad took out the liver – blue-black and long like a snake – the ozone bladders, the valve-bulbs popping like rice bubbles and the heart as big as a volleyball and just as hard, filled with the aerogel blood that had retreated in from the arteries as the fish made its lonely descent. All of it still icy as clouds, we had to keep dipping our hands in a bucket of warm water to stave off frostbite. We washed all the fish bits baptismally and put them into plastic bags: Mr Hiro would probably be willing to pay good money for those too. The weirder it is, the more rich folk want to eat it.

Then came the biggest surprise. "Holy mother of mercy," said Mum as she stepped in to cut behind the green lobes, curtaining a secret pocket of some sort. And like holding a newborn, she extracted the roe sac and laid it solemnly across an ice-covered pillow-case. Ten thousand glowing marbles, all the little moonfish eggs that would never see the darkness of the stratosphere, pulsing slightly, hiding against each other from the glare of the kitchen light such that they churned around like hot miso soup. Or a suitcase filled with diamonds.

Mum and Dad began drafting strategies for bargaining with Mr Hiro, warning that we must approach with tight lips, steady eyes and poker faces, keep our cool. The fascinating thing about a windfall is not so much the joy of good fortune but the perverse fear of its loss, especially when dealing with a jackpot as unfamiliar as this. It hung like a dark pall over everything, again that feeling of tainted joy. The fear, no, the expectation of a monumental screw-up, was never far from the peripheral vision of our optimism.

So, all organs sacredly wrapped and the clean carcass folded into a wet bedsheet, off we went to Mr Hiro. All us kids were scared of Mr Hiro, even though we'd hardly ever seen the guy. We'd just heard things. Smelt things.

His world did not belong to ours, nor ours to his: a subterranean kingdom of flames and steam, with weird things hanging, broiling, pickling and fermenting in jade-coloured aquariums, and any number of plaintive animal sounds, all right at the heel of our block, in some vast gallery only accessible to rich people who knew about strange trapdoors in the pavement, and how to perform the arcane transactions required to procure a piece of some endangered creature no bigger than your thumb, and how to come and go in this dingy part of town without notice. We, the hoi polloi, had never eaten there and never would. We cited moral reasons, always a good cover for the absence of privilege, but the burn of curiosity never left us. Mum and Dad only knew Mr Hiro because of their delivery route. Everyone gets deliveries. Even people like Mr Hiro. Packages that moved and sloshed and squeaked and required a certain discretion, a mutual silence broken only by a few code words, dressed up as idle talk about the weather.

Even so, it took some chin-wagging about storm fronts and sunshine before the surly kitchenhands squatting in the filthy back lane granted us the slightest attention, but in the end simply pulling back that cold, wet bedsheet did wonders for elevating their haunches. They rolled aside a huge bin and ushered us discreetly through a bolted door, eyes as big as dipping bowls. Through the intestinal warren we went, elbows tucked in, manoeuvring our giant fish between chefs as they bustled this way and that, dancers in an ancient rite, flashing knives and flames and stringy ropes of meat; our guide barking abusively and slapping away our wandering fingers, "Touch nothing! Go here! Wait here!" – so worth it to have harangued our parents into letting us come with them. Everyone in the kitchen pretended to regard us as invisibles but we could see them looking sidelong at what we had, and whispering among themselves. Uninvited royalty in a foreign kingdom.

And then, from quiet shapes silhouetted in steam, Mr Hiro came, drifting.

We could sense Mum's jaw tightening, Dad pointlessly smoothing his few strands of hair, as we mentally shielded ourselves from unknown unknowns. What was it about this old man? The one behind the wild rumours, who drew to this cramped labyrinth some of the greatest chefs in the world and towered over them all like a god? Did I mention that he was not quite four feet tall? With the face of a tortoise? A tortoise with really long teeth. He peered up at us, saying nothing, focusing on some indistinct point beyond the top of our heads, an ancient calligraphy of impatience written across his brow. Surrounding staff shrank in size or otherwise made themselves scarce. We bowed, involuntarily, an invisible force of submission at work on our spines. He waved his hand, gesturing at us to lift the damp cloth.

Mr Hiro leant forward and sniffed uninterestedly. With some sleight of hand he produced a small knife from the air and cut a sliver of the moonfish from behind its gill. He pressed it between his fingers like a piece of dough, held it to a hanging light bulb, pressed again, shrugged. "We take," he said, and with a second sleight of hand conjured a small red envelope of cash from somewhere, presented like a plucked flower on upturned palms. Mum reached out gingerly, took it, opened it, counted a very small wad of very small bills, closed it again. She had been practising her poker face so diligently, this sudden and mysterious transaction caught it slipping, right to the floor, lost somewhere between buckets of flapping crustaceans, eels and other things yet to be named by science.

"Um," she said.

Mr Hiro continued to observe us through some distant lens.

"Look," he said in a reedy voice, his finger darting over the body of the fish like a flustered insect. "These parts, no good. This part, no good. This part, two minute ago, maybe OK. Now look, not so OK."

And he was right: the lustrous colour along the edge of the fins was becoming milky grey even as he spoke. The eye, now that we actually looked at it, was more like a boiled egg – a *black* boiled egg. The lips were falling off like gelatinous bucket handles. Em, Jo and Lee held up the iced bags of organs, our iridescent treasures, the great ace up our rooky fishmonger's sleeve, now sweating a very unappealing brown mush, fizzing with sputum, the opposite of gourmet. When had that happened?

What about the roe? The roe! Pim had the roe! But where was Pim? Mr Hiro raised his birdlike hands to the air, dropped his chin, an open apology for every kind of cosmic unfairness.

"Moonfish live in sky," he explained in a weird singsong way. "Shiny, heavenly, perfect creature. Here, this world, they die. Not just the body but everything, soul, spirit, taste, everything die. Customer want to eat moonfish, pay a lot for moonfish, always dream about moonfish. Because customer can't eat moonfish. One hour, two hour, sun come up, all gone. We hurry, rescue little piece here and here. Quickly serve, maybe still good."

He took Mum's hands and gently folded them over the envelope, as you would the ashes of a deceased relative. In that empty beat among the din of pots and pans and huffing flames, the kitchenhands indicated with animated brows the preferable option of an unceremonious exit. The eyes of the old tortoise went big, the mouth a rictus of yellow tombstones, all avuncular kindness expired.

"What else you do?" he growled.

And he was right.

What was a dead fish worth to any of us? Like everything else in the city, only as much as someone would pay for it, and the ever-diminishing window in which that might happen.

Before he disappeared back into his steamy lair, Mr Hiro said one more thing – too high or low for any of us to make out – and then laughed, a raking birdlike sound that still rings in our ears to this day. The kitchen-hands heaved our moonfish and all its sundry organs down some narrow stairway, toward the sound of sharpening knives and clinking glass, and we never saw that poor creature again. Well, not all of it. We still didn't know where Pim had gotten to.

*

Pim, as any of us would have guessed earlier if we'd bothered to squander a moment and think about it, was right back where it had started, such was his wordless way. When we all finally came up roofside, there he was:

a small dark frame perched atop the air conditioning duct, wafting moonfish eggs one by one back up into the sky. We all got up there to help him, Mum and Dad included, crouching in the dark, elbow-deep once more in freezing piscine mucous as if we couldn't get enough of it. How much do I love our family? This much. When nothing turns out to be what we hoped, we still hope it turns out to be something. We are never ones to say that life is disappointing. We are always too busy doing stuff, even if we have no idea why.

And yes, it was strange to think about that moonfish mother vanishing into some underground purgatory, the pawn of some trade either fair or wretched, and how late it was that we came to put away our thrills and feel sorry for such a crime as we had done, while these eggs, these tiny eggs that constantly pulsed upwards and spun like marbles, were now more vibrant and alive than when we'd first unsheathed them. No sooner did we cup each one in our hands than the small moonfish fry seemed to grow and pop out of their liquid casings, staining our clothes with yet more heavenly muck, wriggling up into that cool and bottomless mystery that always hangs unbidden above our heads. So quickly they went, just like shooting stars, once they got wind of their bearings, long before the rousing dawn of the city could fade their shine completely. And so, here it was, the third great gift of the moonfish: an upward shower of golden sparks, a benediction of transcendental caviar, and remorse.

So, you may ask, after all that, do we still go fishing? Yes, we do. If the wind is right, the fire escapes clear, the moon in the right phase. We just like sitting around in the dark doing next to nothing. Feeling the vibration of wind on a dumb thread, searching for that telltale scatter of fish eyes in the night sky until our arses feel like pincushions, our stomachs growl and our eyelids call it quits. So what if we forget to bait our hooks and never catch a thing? Like I said, stupidity or fun.

The rhino was on the motorway again.

We blew our horns in outrage!
Men came, shot it dead, pushed it to one side.
We blew our horns in gratitude!

But that was yesterday.
Today we all feel terrible.
Nobody knew it was the last rhino.
How could we have known it was the last one?

I'm not afraid of the waiting room,
the way it always smells like waiting
as the world goes on outside without me.

I'm not afraid of doctors and nurses,
their friendly soft footfalls down long corridors,
quiet as unspoken facts.

I'm not afraid of antiseptic rooms, of theatres.
I like the brightness. I like the benevolent round edges.
Clean metal and linen.
They are ready to take me in now.

The strange machines, I know them all.
Kind voices always explain everything,
the tubes and lights and drips and clicks.
There is nothing to worry about. I know, I know.

But still, there it is, always waiting.

White on white, soft feathers can't hide
the black needle tips.
I listen to what they are always telling me and try not to look,
even as I stretch out my naked arm.

Accept it, I tell myself, accept the weight
of big claws stepping up.
Breathe, keep breathing
as they grasp my skin.

Now higher, high on my shoulder.
Resist the urge to run.

Breathe, keep breathing, as it settles on my chest,
talons on my collarbone
and they say: you may feel a pressure.
And so it comes.
Wings expand around my ears, filling the room.

I promised myself I would not cry, I promised
even as the arctic heartbeat thrums
against my tight-shut eyes,
even when it feels like I'm drowning in feathers.

Think that friends and family will be here soon
letting me know how brave I am.
How strong.
Think of warm hands and safe words,
flowers and cards,
hopes and wishes.

And later, try not to look to the other side of the bed,
how it stays behind when all visitors have left,
softly breathing in and out
with nothing to say.

Ignore the click of talons on the railing.
Ignore the big lighthouse eyes that turn to stare
and turn away again,
as if casting over a void.

It will never know my name.
It will never know how I feel.
It only knows one thing,
one cold fact forever guarded in silence:
In time you will be well.

Until then the owl will never leave my side.
It will caress me the only way it can,
with claws and feathers and stares
and every time I reach out to it in fear
I reach out in gladness,
because owls are never wrong.

One afternoon the members of the board all turned into frogs. You might say they had it coming, but that's not what this story is about. This story is about the person who found them like that.

Summoned to enter the boardroom only by silence, the sudden and unnerving cessation of the usual profane shouting, the secretary saw them floundering and gasping all over the varnished mahogany, tiny frogs, one per board member, each about the size of a plum. She recoiled in horror, shut the double doors, returned to her desk, played solitaire on her computer for about a minute. Then, feeling ashamed, she re-entered the boardroom. The executives were still frogs, some now flopped on their backs, waving their limbs uselessly in the air. She righted them gently.

The touch of their skin was not unpleasant – it was delicate and soft, a little sticky maybe. The untouched water glasses beckoned on the table, and she used them to give each amphibian a sprinkling of moisture, dipping her hand, flicking her fingers, moving to the next one, dipping and flicking, as if the endless ritual of putting out water glasses all these years had been for such an unforeseen occurrence as this. She circled and circled, administering her bizarre baptismal hydration, she didn't know what else to do, or who to call. She was worried that she wouldn't be believed. Or worse, blamed. Fired. The police might even be involved. That's what happens to people like me, she thought grimly.

Since the recession, even the tiniest bit of trouble would mean losing everything. The latent nightmare of this hung above her head every waking hour, she was thinking of it even when she wasn't thinking of it. That's something that the wealthy don't understand about the rest of us, she thought, that our world is constant worry about money. We are the ones who worry, who prop up the world with our worry. They think it is the other way around, doing the things that they do, as if that's the natural order, top to bottom. But there's no natural order, it's all luck and absurdity, it's up and down and upside down, the place you were born, the colour of your face, the debt you inherit before you're even pushed out. She thought about her brother, the impulsive thing he had or had not done, so tiny under the shadow of those vast crimes premeditated in cool, high offices, the play that set the game for every other misdemeanour to follow. She knew, she heard things, being the human furniture that served coffee, took memos, aligned leather desk pads, whose name could never be properly pronounced or even remembered in the first place. Oh, it made her so angry! She was flicking water hard on the frogs now and the frogs were flinching. She stopped, apologized, quietened her mind. Maybe she was being unfair. Maybe she too was guilty of making the same dumb assumptions that had led to every other collapse, of not seeing people as people, with all their fragility, fear and complicated weakness, amphibious or otherwise. She remembered how her mother had always lectured about forgiveness, and she tried hard to forgive, and it worked, it actually worked. A cool wave descended, a calm distance. She felt immediately better. But the members of the board were still frogs. What to do about that? She would have to get rid of them somehow, and soon, before anyone else came in and started asking questions.

What had she done as a child, in those distant days in the old place, when she found a frog? There had been plenty around. "Back to the swamp!" her mother had yelled – compassion always had limits – and she returned them dutifully, naming each as she went in those brief moments they had to form friendships. But all the wetlands around here were now choked by the effluent of the very corporation she worked for, dead for years, frequented only by plastic bags and other things too vile to be named: it was cheaper to pay fines than fix infrastructure. And the alley cats, misshapen spectres that they were, devoured almost anything catchable in the rank shade of dustbins. How like the spirit of our times, she thought. Maybe she could take them home, keep them in a bath or something. No, a tank of some kind. An aquarium! One with lovely rocks and moss and cool trickling water and a log and little warming lights and tiny fish to keep them company. She had seen such a thing in a department store once and the thought excited her in a way she hadn't known since she was a child, standing up to her knees in the holy bliss of mud. It was like a bloom of oxygenated water, a thrill whose very triviality was thrilling, so ridiculous and wonderful and secret. Just as quickly as this feeling came it transmuted into words, the first she had ever dared to utter within this space. "I will look after these frogs," she pledged to a room whose only ears were small, indented and olive-green, "no matter what!"

As for the frogs, the former members of the board, flailing against the slippery table top as they stretched out brand new legs and tongues, tested the lightness of their little triangular hearts, they had never known such overwhelming joy, such release. The universe had not cursed them, it had pardoned them. The secretary picked them up one by one and put them carefully into her handbag.

"Respect the sheep," the teacher told us, "We owe it so much. The wool that keeps us warm, the meat that feeds us, even the milk, the bones and skin, all worth more to this city than gold." And respect it we did, lining up, taking turns to press an ear to its hot woolly body, trembling with animal life, something much bigger than any lesson. We whispered the words we'd learned by rote and let the musty smell of rain-washed fleece fill our noses.

But it was not enough to block the rank breeze that rolled in from the port: the gigantic livestock ship loading against an ill-timed easterly. We knew everyone would be rushing to get the laundry off the line, cancelling al fresco dinners, evening strolls, patio parties, outdoor swims. It was so awful, even with all the classroom windows closed. Thank God the bell rang. "Respect the sheep!" cried the teacher as we bustled roughly out of the room, his voice desperate, breaking. We tried hard to think of something else, something good, like the simple fact of missing out on homework as we left him there, hugging that poor sheep.

The boy was a genius! That's what the newspapers said. That's what his parents told the newspapers. That's what the boy had dutifully demonstrated for his parents. And who among the countless audiences that followed could doubt it?

He began talking at four months, could read at five months and play a fair game of chess a few weeks later. At two he knew the atlas by heart, at three he was doing the family accounts; no small task given so many estates and holdings. By his fifth birthday he could speak eight languages, including one he invented. He sang songs he'd composed in all of them as he blew out the candle flames, then returned upstairs to discover a new comet using a self-constructed telescope. His parents glowed, their radical teaching methods finally celebrated instead of lampooned. It was time to open every door to the world.

What a marvel! A prodigy for our time! Journalists jostled for an exclusive. Bulbs flashed. What is it like to be the youngest person ever admitted to university? Is it true that you built a fusion reactor the size of a walnut in your own bedroom? Wrote an opera? Devised a new theory of gravity? Identified a vaccine to save the lives of millions, using nothing more than pencil, paper and your local library? Of all the great mysteries of the universe, of all the problems afflicting the world, which will you turn your brilliant gaze upon next?

The boy answered as best he could, even as his mind roamed elsewhere, probing with childlike energy the strange, scintillating dimensions of a world into which he had been born.

Editors hammered their articles into shape, shaking their heads in wonder. What the human mind could achieve at such an age! An inspiration to all! They wrote about his shirt, the colour of his eyes, his unique walking style. They even wrote about his dreams: visions of molecular structures, falling apples, mathematical proofs written across the sky, epic sonatas. A brilliant mind that never rests! An engine of unimaginable potential! As if anyone could know such things. As if speculation might harden into fact through nothing more than the drying of ink.

In truth, the boy never spoke about his dreams, not even to his parents, not that his parents ever asked. It was the one part of his life that required no proof nor demonstration, no verification, no audience, and he longed to keep it that way, not least because it was the one part of life that also seemed utterly beyond explanation.

What did he dream about?

He dreamt about hippos.

He only ever dreamt about hippos.

There were about six of them, maybe more, just under the slow-moving river that cascaded over their big smooth backs. There were lily pads and bees. There was a hum of muddy eternity, a prickly heat, all hazed in dust and light, vibrant. In the dream, the hippos turned to him languidly and waggled their funny-looking ears. It made him giggle like an infant every time. Then he would wake up.

The dream always faded so quickly, seemed so pointless and meaningless. An obfuscation of reason that stole precious hours of consciousness, time in which one could properly think and work: this is what his parents had once remarked over a high-protein breakfast, and like them, the boy practised a method of sleeping for under four hours a day. He still dreamt about hippos, but far less. His academic achievements soared in inverse proportion. The world stood transfixed.

The men from the government turned up more and more often. As did the men from the newspapers, in one instance grabbing him by the jacket collar to yank him in front of a camera as he walked home from the campus where he taught students twice his own age. In the ensuing scuffle – or "wild lashing out" as it was later reported – the journalist fell and hit his head, badly. Charges were laid, headlines struck. Rumours circulated of a nervous breakdown, a thing the media seemed to have been waiting upon, secretly expecting and even, perversely, hoping for. Behold the troubled prodigy, the socially maladjusted savant, the freak! The government men came again, offering certain protections, opportunities. They presented the boy with papers, scenarios, patriotic sermons, icy threats and warm reassurances.

The boy said no.

His parents recoiled.

Life became difficult.

Far away a war was looming and it cast a very long shadow. Public opinion soured further when the boy presented public lectures about a political system that would end all militarized conflict, a fiscal system that gave a commercial index to moral virtue, and a world without religion. He was booed offstage. During a protest march he was beaten by police. He spent some time in prison. The government men offered no help this time. Neither did his parents.

Small mercies, he thought.

For the journalists, this was all a matter of passing and diminishing interest; little more than an obituary for a person not quite deceased enough to warrant a headline. Pity the child genius, they wrote, his every shining star has fallen out of orbit. Potential squandered, promises betrayed. And so the boy was forgotten, or else his name became a kind of cautionary shorthand for spectacular failure.

It wasn't until many years later that a journalist tracked down the boy wonder (as they still called the forty-year-old man) for a *'Where Are They Now?'* special in a popular magazine. The young woman had a kind and sympathetic manner, so much so that her subject relaxed his lifelong hatred for the press and returned, just for a moment, to his true nature: open, friendly, ebullient.

He detailed all his menial jobs in quiet satellite cities, places with names that nobody cared to remember, wanting only a fair day's pay, to be left alone, to be allowed to think and study in peace. He told her how employers invariably wondered about the odd lilt of his voice, maybe saw a picture in an old clipping, or recalled one of the many TV performances arranged by his parents; how the same employers would promote him to a senior management position, hoping to profit from the windfall of his genius; how he would then quit, change his name, and move on, condemned as ungrateful. How he still worked prodigiously on his own theories, designs, inventions, publishing papers under different pseudonyms in obscure journals. He did his best to explain each of them in layperson's terms.

The journalist listened with genuine interest, admired his simple but tidy apartment, his collection of colourful diodes and electrical insulators, his companion budgerigars that perched on every light fitting, flying down to preen behind his ears from time to time.

Yes, he was very happy. The happiest he had ever been.

No, he did not want to talk about his parents.

No pictures, thank you.

She did not ask about his dreams.

Someone brought the article into the factory a few months later, he knew even before he could hear them laughing upstairs. They read aloud the details of his "mindless" work history, his "autistic" prattling, his "miserable" garret-aviary. Further, the article mocked every revelation of his life's work: his logarithmic table of odours, the endless maps of cumulus clouds drawn in small notebooks, the "crackpot" theory of water memory, the design of a machine for the recovery of bird calls that may have happened over a century ago but which, the once-celebrated genius maintained, still sustained the weakest of observable vibrations in the air around us. How mad, wrote the journalist, how eccentric. How sad.

And how unsurprising – for this is what the article implied above all else. As if to remind the reader that any supernatural talent comes at great cost, a thing the rest of us are spared. As if the thought of being ordinary becomes its own reassurance. Pity the exceptional.

And when the factory staff jostled their way to the basement in search of their quarry, to hold the photograph against the man himself, there was nothing to greet them but silence, an empty desk and a hot cup of tea.

The letters of history will tell us that he again changed his name and moved away, make mention of a cerebral hemorrhage, or pills, as if speculation might eventually harden into facts if left unstirred. And so it did.

But consider for a moment that these are only words on paper, that in truth there was no body, living or dead, and possibly there never had been one. There was nothing to fill the funerary cloth woven by the media, and when every crease of curiosity had been starched and ironed flat, the only thing left to fold and bury was a name. A word that nobody could remember, that had barely existed in the first place, and invited no eulogy.

Elsewhere, the hum of insects and tropical heat pressed in upon his ears, and he waggled them. He felt his own girth and the girth of those beside him, and the weightless mass of water that touched everything that ever existed, rank and sweet with the knowledge of all things living and dead. The hippos opened their wide, wide mouths to let it in and together they slipped beneath the surface.

We found them in gutters, drainpipes, any place with water, which in the days after the hurricanes was pretty much everywhere. So many pooled at the foot of subway stairs as to bring to mind a failed salmon migration. But such remarkable things barely gave us pause during the clean-up. Too much had happened, too much turmoil and damage and sorrow, so that our exhausted, waterlogged hearts were immune to all marvels, and we moved through endless vales of sleet like machines, or rather like ghosts. All things foamed and fogged and our minds slept where they stood. There was always more shovelling to do.

So we simply picked them up, all those slippery lungfish, and took them with us in plastic bags, not a breath lost on comment. We all knew which lungfish belonged to which worker, of course, you only had to check their faces; and yes, it was their faces that ultimately saved them from the dull blade of a shovel and awakened some faint spark of feeling in us all. I don't know how else to say this: they had our faces. The same eyes, noses, mouths … it was crazy. Not knowing what else to do, we filled tubs and baths and laundry sinks once we'd finally gotten home and knocked the mud from our boots. In the dog-tired moments before collapsing in a heap, we dutifully read up on what you were supposed to feed a lungfish. Fish food, apparently.

Only in the morning solitude of bathrooms did our aching heads have a moment to take them in and reel. We observed the hypnotic beauty of those primeval things, black and languid in the stillness, fins pressed down against the pressure of passing time, all peaceful and leafy, and we wondered aloud, "What the hell?"

But explanation is a luxury we can't afford these days, and reality doesn't care for it, being far too busy following its own unknowable course. So when the lungfish grew small limbs and clambered out of the water, yearning for the air and light of other rooms, you might have called it progress or evolution, or you might have called it a meaningless accident of nature or nothing at all, in the wordless, jaw-gaping language of watery things. Nobody cared either way. The amphibians – as this was what they now seemed to be – were watching TV on a couch beside us soon enough, and when the city's fish food supplies ran out they just ate leftovers from our own plates. Their little faces remained the same, quite pallid and expressionless, neither creepy nor endearing, like looking at your reflection in a still pond: *oh yes, there I am*. They moved their weak forelimbs in sympathy as we lifted a fork or changed the channel. Those would later become hands, of course, and their newly lidded eyes began to track us as we moved from room to room, following every domestic ritual with intense, cool-blooded interest.

When they stood upright, lost their tails and beckoned for clothes... yes, you could say that it was a little disconcerting. But nothing of it felt odd, and we didn't think of them as strange creatures. They were just our other selves, and we recognized in their soft smiles and stares a subtlety of character that even our closest friends and family would find invisible or uninteresting. Was our fascination parental or narcissistic? Was it curiosity or devotion? Was there any point asking? They were here and needed us to look after them, and we gladly obliged. Gladly, because even as they changed and changed again there was something dependable about their presence, grasping our knees gently, an absurd anchorage in a deluged, gale-force world. We felt it most acutely when leaving each grey day for work, our joints aching before the first shift had even started.

When they began to help around our apartments, we were grateful, and corrected all their mistakes. Before long our shirts were ironed perfectly, some for the first time ever. The smell of burning in the kitchen came to be replaced with wonderful and exotic aromas – who knew you could do such things with celery? – and all faulty hinges, washers and bulbs were, after years of neglect, suddenly fixed. It's hard to convey how natural it all seemed, and how even the first conversations began without us really noticing. Just a word here and there, a few agreeable nods, a chuckle over a shared joke. We always had to bend low to hear them, though, as their voices were so tiny, and their bodies, while becoming more humanlike, did not get any bigger. If anything, they were getting smaller. You might see them busy with nail scissors and needles in the night, readjusting the clumsy infant onesies we had given them and appearing at first light dressed in smart suits, ready to serve tiny green pancakes beside a newspaper already read from front to back and ironed flat again, with salient details highlighted in fluorescent pen. Their editorial skills were stunning. And those pancakes! Oh, how we miss them now.

Needless to say, they weren't living in bathrooms or laundries by this time. They had built their own cosy domiciles in the spaces we'd ignored, gaps between shelves or under coffee tables, with a staggering knack for architectural economy and recycling of rubbish. Designs no human had ever laid eyes on, and yet not at all unfamiliar. The other selves were so much like us in every downscaled respect, and the sense of kinship only deepened as we conversed late into the night, as was our habit back then. They essentially did what we did, only better, and yes, they wanted what we wanted, only more so.

When they started going to work full time, they prioritized and accomplished every task with a logic that inspired in us both pride and embarrassment. Pride at seeing our other selves shine so brightly, embarrassment about our own faded to-do lists and unmet ideals. While we watched sitcoms in the evening, wearily munching on unethical dinners, they were reading up on physics and history, and even presented illustrated lectures on climate change in our lounge rooms, complete with handout notes and feedback forms. They were never offended when we fell asleep to flickering images of global disaster and plaintive calls for action, even after they'd listened to our own personal gripes all day – things so trivial we could tell no one else – with patient gifts of sympathy and tiny hand-patting. They would just pack up their projectors and return to upgraded apartments, now built among beautiful vertical gardens spread across our exterior walls, or visit rooftop libraries and research labs, with doors too small for us, the bigger selves, to enter. Not that we even thought to, being so busy with our own affairs. And frankly, too tired.

Perhaps because of this unspoken divide, our other selves soon had lives of their own, a whole new city woven carefully through the fabric of the old. You might see threadlike beams of gold darting about your ankles, transmitting the collected energies of dew and sunlight between miniature schools, hospitals and embassies, or observe their vehicles slipping beneath our own gridlock like a school of quicksilver sardines, oblivious to any flash flood. Knee-high shopping arcades sparkled like diamonds in the narrow canyons between our bland public buildings, everything for free but nothing we could use, and bright new tunnels webbed their way under filthy railway platforms. Mysterious objects crept into art gallery stairwells, of far more interest than the galleries themselves, and in the spare corners of cinemas you might see the diminutive glow of those other movies, our other selves crowded about them on plush chairs. How we secretly longed to sit in front of those odd little films, fluttering with mysterious beauty and wordless drama, a single glance of which reduced our own big-screen entertainments to nothing more than a formulaic and juvenile spectacle. Oh, certainly, we did feel some envy, jealousy and even hostility, but all our distempers only ever returned to the same neutralizing thought: they were, after all, us.

And we were they. Might we have been inspired to do better ourselves? We should have been, yes, we should have. There was just something about all their public forums, fundraisers, awareness campaigns, think tanks and action groups, all those palm-sized journals of critical review, all that upbeat righteousness, that desire to make us better people... Well, it induced a kind of misery only surpassed by the bad weather. Every brilliant scheme just made us feel terrible, every shining paragon only deepened a perverse resolve to find comfort in old habits and traditions, to "be ourselves", a phrase that had itself become so maddeningly confusing. Maybe this is what our young doppelgängers failed to understand. They believed their good example would be enough. That just being right was enough. They knew nothing about injured pride or the true inertia of human nature. They didn't know how to speak to us.

Now it all seems like a string of receding impressions, falling back into the rain each time we turn away to wipe our brows. Their miniature planes on airport tarmacs no bigger than a single parking space, powered by lentil-green batteries farmed in the sea, grew smaller and smaller. We heard less about their remarkable health systems, their moneyless economy, their conceptually bizarre – but undeniably effective – plan for world peace. Presumably that was all still unfolding somewhere else, just becoming ever smaller, turning inwards, until it was all too infinitesimal for us to see.

But we do sense them, we know they are there, somewhere in the microcosmic vibrations of wires and bloodstreams, a tangle of chromosomes, all those other selves. The ones we first met as poor lungfish gasping in the gutters of our crisis, who mirrored our good intentions so diligently, and who saw in our wind-blasted, bone-weary compassion a great hope for the future, right at the moment we bent down to pick them up.

We took the orca from the sea and put it in the sky. It was just so beautiful up there, so inspiring. But the calls of the mother never stopped. From a cold and foreign sea, her subsonic wavelength penetrated all concrete, steel and urban clamour, reverberated through pipes and sewers, kept us awake all night and broke our hearts. We knew we had done something unforgivable. We promised to set things right. But so many years have passed, and the mother is still calling out. So many years have passed and the orca is still in the sky. We just don't know how to get it down.

You will never escape the tiger. The tiger will always find you. It will follow you for a long time, without you even knowing, just waiting for the perfect moment to strike. Hours it will follow. Days, weeks, years … a whole lifetime can go by; the tiger is a patient animal! But when it does finally decide the time is right to leap, to embrace you in its furry arms, to seize you by the neck and drag you back into the very jungle you came from, even then you will not see it coming because the tiger only ever attacks from behind.

But there is a simple solution to this problem, so simple as to be almost laughable. Just wear a mask on the back of your head.

Any kind of mask will do. The more garish the better. Our research clearly shows that a second face, worn like this, is more effective than any other known protection. It is very easy to do, costs almost nothing, and you can make one yourself at home. It can even be a fun rainy-day activity: papier mâché, egg-cartons, rubber bands, paint, glitter and glue. Anything will do.

Of course, the tiger is smart. Very smart. It will probably learn the secret of your simple ruse eventually. But the tiger is also a very, very careful animal. An impeccable hunter. The one great weakness of this animal is perfectionism. Even the tiniest whisker of doubt will freeze its every muscle, still its every breath, fix its eyeballs like glass beads just long enough for that lethal moment to pass. It will then immediately retreat to stalking at a safe distance. You cannot avoid the tiger, no, but you can make it hesitate. Confuse it a little. Not for long enough to avoid death, of course, but certainly long enough for you to enjoy a good and meaningful life, which is all any of us can reasonably ask for.

But here is the real problem. Most people – even those who have read all the literature, who know the facts, who agree with the facts – will refuse to wear a mask on the back of their heads. Even when it could save their lives! Perhaps it's one more thing they have to remember to put on every day, to carry around, to not leave behind in a bathroom. Perhaps, like all the best preventative measures, it achieves no perceptible result, which can sometimes be mistaken for not working at all, a very common and, alas, often fatal human error. Perhaps many do not believe the tiger is really there, but that it has gone away, that it is extinct. Our survey subjects have given all these reasons. None are true.

The truth is this: a mask on the back of your head looks absolutely ridiculous.

Unless everybody is wearing such a thing, almost nobody will. This is a great weakness of humankind. We are very self-conscious, easily embarrassed and, much like the tiger, generally want to look as respectable as possible all the time, especially in public. But unlike the tiger, who knows in its heart of hearts that stripes are the best thing in the world and would never conceive questioning its own appearance under any circumstances – not even if it meant death – humans are not so sure about such things. Many of our rules concerning appearance and behaviour come from a place quite far away from our own hearts. We are endlessly torn between what we want to do and what others expect of us, and more often than not defer to the latter.

Accordingly, the majority of subjects who tried the mask, who dabbled with the wild absurdity of it and even liked it, eventually returned to ordinary life, sans mask, at the behest of social pressures. The backs of their heads remain completely exposed, or poorly compensated with a tasteful hat or well-styled cut, neither of which means a thing to the tiger (in fact it only helps the tiger track you in a crowd). The unprotected tend to reserve this one consoling thought: if there are enough people around, the tiger will choose somebody else, not me. Especially in a big city, the probability of a tiger attack must surely approach zero. The tiger can only eat so much! Unfortunately, the statistics do not bear this out. But here we come to yet another human weakness: a great difficulty in putting facts before intuition. Lives continue to be needlessly lost. Especially in big cities.

So, what about those few subjects who do, in spite of all odds, persist in wearing a mask? That is the most interesting finding of all our research. After a few years of committed adornment, these subjects reported diminished anxiety in relation to how ridiculous they look. They reported diminished anxiety in relation to what people say or think about them. They reported diminished anxiety in relation to a great many other things too. At the same time, their masks have become bigger, more ornate, more startling and outlandish, and not necessarily for the purpose of bewildering the tiger any more. In fact, if you can convince one of these committed users that the tiger is no longer a threat, they still keep wearing the mask!

Of course, it comes at great cost. These same subjects have also lost jobs, friends, lovers, the respect of communities; they've been verbally abused on public transport, denied service in restaurants, expelled from religious and educational institutions, even harassed by the police. And all for just wearing an unusual head covering! Not that the mask is ever mentioned explicitly. But then again, feelings of contempt are never well concealed among humans. Like the tiger, we are skilled in the art of passive aggression. Unlike the tiger, we use it almost exclusively against our own kind. The committed mask-wearers know this well, but have long stopped caring. They have come to learn that the rules of human society are frequently absurd, that mutual respect may not be possible, that in some cases, it's better to live by one's own rules instead. Just like the tiger: proud and free.

On that note, one final and very interesting observation. Without exception, all of the long-term mask-wearers studied keep an image of their predator nearby, visible at all times. Tattoos, desk ornaments, garden statues, vast wall hangings, diamond-encrusted brooches and in one case a private jet painted in orange and black stripes. Should you ask why, they will all tell you the same thing, as if it is the simplest thing in the world: *I have learned to love the tiger.*

People who don't live with parrots always ask the same question of those who do: *can your parrot talk?* That's because humans love talking. From the cradle to the grave our lives are measured, trimmed, emboldened by words, and to hear another animal speak them back to us is nothing short of pure delight. Can we call it language? Or just some parlour-trick illusion? Maybe it doesn't matter one way or another. Maybe it's enough to feel we are not entirely alone in our funny little world of words, spinning through the big dark universe as we are. And that's why people – people who don't live with parrots – always want to know if a parrot can talk.

People who don't live with parrots always ask if a parrot can do tricks. That's because humans love tricks. So, as it happens, do parrots. They can do almost anything with their feet that a human can, boasting twice the number of opposable thumbs. And while our own feeble mouths can barely crack a nut, a parrot's beak is a miracle of engineering: an ingenious hook-and-chisel vice forged in an age of thundering reptiles, with all the sensitivity and grace missing from a handyman's toolbox. In some other universe of geological twists, it may well have been parrots building great technological empires and taking primates as pets, training them to speak parrot, do parrot tricks… should they have evolved such wayward and unnecessary interests.

People who don't live with parrots will always marvel at the familiarity of their intelligence, their playful curiosity, their friendly faces bright with intention and knowing smiles, their anthropomorphic little souls. Look at how they move their feet in time to music! The way they cock their head to one side! *They are just like you and me!*

So say the people who don't live with parrots.

As for us, the people who *do* live with parrots, we see no such reflection in nature's mirror. Behind those small, mercurial eyes that stare so fiercely into the noonday sun without flinching, there clicks a primeval arithmetic that grants no access. When happy a parrot will grind its beak angrily. When angry it will dance happily. It bites us with enough affection to draw blood, and the most sacred gifts of devotion are delivered as vomit. And even for such inverted expression all these chauvinistically human words – "happiness", "anger", "devotion" – are just meaningless chaff in the breeze. They are nothing compared to the squawk of a parrot, blanching our eardrums like a morning prayer straight out of the Jurassic, allowing no room for translation or reply. A parrot asks for neither. A parrot has already stolen our food, defecated on our shoulder and flown off to find something more interesting.

But when that same parrot returns, leans in against our face to preen hair and eyebrows – our sorry excuse for feathers – it does so with such surprising tenderness. Can we call it love? Yes, let's call it love. The parrot will not mind, it will let us think whatever we want. Its heart trembles against our cheek like tiny jungle drums, the earth turns once again on its billion-year axis, and we think quietly to ourselves: *what a strange privilege it is to be here, now, and living with a parrot.*

Bears with lawyers.

It was as simple and terrible as that.

For the first time in a very long while, longer than anyone could remember, or wanted to remember, the bears were able to speak through legal representatives: men and women in black gowns who studied Ursine and held aloft the hefty paperwork that allowed their clients to walk freely through the city without being shot. And walk they did, right past armed police and animal-control officers, past bewildered motorists and pedestrians, workers and shoppers, right into our great halls of justice.

Humankind was being sued, it turned out. A class action of epic proportions: *Ursidae vs Homo sapiens.*

That wasn't the worst of it.

Human Law is not the only legal system on the planet, it turned out. There are as many systems as there are species, the lawyers for the bears explained to an incredulous room, under which all animals are recognized as legal entities within a cosmic hierarchy. Human Law isn't even very high on this hierarchy (apparently we are just below Walrus Law) and Bear Law actually takes precedence in most cases. The fact that we didn't know any of this only seemed to strengthen the bears' case at the expense of our own.

Shaken? Yes, but hardly worried, and we are not ones to flinch. We had the best legal team that money could buy and immediately launched our broadside. *We do not recognize so-called Bear Law! No such nonsense has ever existed! You have nothing to show us!*

And so the bears showed us.

Sure enough, there it was as plain as day, in all the places we never bothered to look: on the tailfins of freshwater trout, under the bark of trees, in the creased silt of riverbeds, on the wing-scale of moths and butterflies, in the cursive coastlines of entire continents. Moss, sand, dew, the arrangement of seeds in a berry, pollen, bacteria, everything. Put a single slice of any rock under the right light and it is all there, literally written in stone. It was humbling, beautiful, indisputable and horrifying. It was all those things. Especially for a legal team that had spent their entire working life in a city, who knew nothing more than the contents of human filing cabinets and libraries. Which were only ever written by humans, it turned out. And meant very little to the rest of the world, it turned out.

That wasn't the worst of it.

Lawyers for the bears now presented us with all the translated paperwork we had requested, stacks of it in huge boxes, boxes that filled shipping containers, shipping containers that sat on the back of trucks,

trucks lined up in a convoy, as far as the eye could see. The city's traffic ground to a halt as they backed one by one into the streets of our brightest legal firms, every fluorescent light and mahogany veneer trembling. If that sight was not demoralizing enough, reading any fraction of the material, a case against humankind gathered over some ten thousand years, was an exercise in abject despair. *Theft. Pillage. Unlawful Occupation. Deportation. Slavery. Murder. Torture. Genocide.* Not to mention all the crimes we'd never even heard of, things like *Spiritual Exclusion*, *Groaking* and *Ungungunurumunre.*

"For the hungriest of all animals," said the bears in their typically abstruse legal verse, "the only thing left to eat is the truth." As if to prove their point, none of our lawyers could view the supporting library of video evidence without losing their lunch.

We countersued, appealed, sought injunctions, mined every technicality and loophole, hiring and firing our own lawyers like there was no tomorrow. We were trumped each time, the bears always sitting so silent and resolute in the upper gallery. How we came to detest their calm, round shapes and sad black eyes. The extent to which we loathed their lawyers we could not even begin to express. Who were these people? They turned our every argument against us, each time presenting some precedent of Bear Law as old and unbreakable as time, dragging various bits of primeval forest into the courtroom. Again and again they exposed the shallowness of every Human Law as presumption, ignorance and hubris.

That wasn't the worst of it.

Deep in our hearts we knew they were right. Even as we fought our defence with such intellectual ferocity, as if to convince ourselves more than our opponents of a truth mired in self-contradiction, we knew the end was coming. It was time to reach a settlement. We called in every favour and came up with a figure that made our eyes water and our mouths dry, a figure too staggering to ever make public.

"Your money is meaningless to us," said the bears. "You grasp economics with the same clawless paws you use for fumbling justice."

And, once again, the bears showed us.

There they were, God help us, the Ledgers of the Earth, written in clouds and glaciers and sediments, tallied in the colours of the sun and the moon as light passed through the millennial sap of every living thing, and we looked upon it all with dread. Ours was not the only fiscal system in the world, it turned out. And worse, our debt was severe beyond reckoning. And worse than worse, all the capital we had accrued throughout history was a collective figment of the human imagination: every asset, stock and dollar. We owned nothing. The bears asked us to relinquish our hold on all that never belonged to us in the first place.

Well, this we simply could not do.

So we shot the bears.

All perfectly legal, it turned out, thanks to a bill passed in the dead of night. We took care of their lawyers too, in a manner we are not at liberty to divulge. But we did ask them, before they went, "Why on earth did you do it? How could you, yourselves human beings, with homes and families and communities, represent those bears, speak for them, support litigation against your own species?"

"We had no choice," they said. "We are sworn to uphold justice."

Oh, please. Humans always have a choice: is that not what makes us unique? And is silence not a form of pcace? We'll never understand why it is so difficult for some people to accept the hard truth of the world. Why they fight, even when they know they cannot win.

And so, finally, finally, finally, things went back to normal.

Until now.

Until now, when the whole sorry and sordid experience with those damned bears comes flooding back. Blood is leeching from every face in the boardroom, and we can already hear the sound of document trucks reversing into streets. A fetid cloud descends over the city, the sickening stench of endless torment and persecution.

"The cattle are here," a terrified receptionist quavers over the intercom, "with lawyers."

In Zürich, I see it. In Sydney, Tokyo, New York, Dubai, Mexico City, Cairo and every stop thereafter. Hopping along corridors. Perching on stainless steel rafters. On top of flight information screens, no less. And nobody says a thing.

"Look," I say, bewildered, "an eagle!"

Other transit passengers glance up, nod, return to devices, reinsert earphones. More casually now, hoping to provoke actual conversation, I persist: "How about that eagle?" And when that fails to elicit anything, "Nice eagle, big wings, sharp beak," by which time I'm basically just prattling to myself. Airport staff, obliged by salary, respond with the standard refrain: "How may we help you?"

Further into my itinerary I see it catching things – lord knows where *they* have come from. A brown rabbit darting behind a vending machine, a lizard on the departure mezzanine, what looks like a wallaby – a wallaby? – fatally befuddled by an upward escalator flowing downwards. The eagle dispatches each blur to quiet corners with a great beat of its wings, plucking fur and tendon in grisly privacy. I simply do what everyone else does, give each incident a wide berth, try not to get any blood on the wheels of my carry-on. *Sheesh, those talons.* I now walk around holding a rolled-up magazine in my hand like a baton, just in case.

It's always a relief to get back on every plane, away from each terminal. Seat belt buckled low and firm. Emergency information card so cleanly illustrated in my hands. But as I decompress into yet another jet-lagged haze upon lift-off, my mouth hangs open and somewhere in the back of my throat there unclouds the strange vision, always the same, of a tiny, tiny airport. And above that tiny airport is a sky, an enormous blue bowl, and within that enormity flies the eagle, its beak open in an endless silent cry. Deep inside its throat I see a desert, hot and vast and flecked with green and red. Above that desert flies a plane. Through the window of that plane – this plane – I see myself, sleeping, mouth open and there it is, another tiny, tiny airport. I wake as the plane shudders against a runway, clueless as usual to the time, place, day of the week, lifting my head from the shoulder of yet another nonplussed stranger.

When I see the eagle at the next terminal I'm determined to think less of it. Surely it's an apparition brought on by the effects of travelling ten thousand metres into the air at two hundred metres per second, squeezing days and stretching nights, stepping from one country to the next through plane fuselage, walkway, conveyor belt and terminal corridor, as if they are all one big, long, hermetically sealed tunnel transporting the body faster than the speed of the mind, faster than belief or imagination, faster than the soul. How I'd love to get some decent rest, ground my ions to something other than carpet or steel, return to that gently turning earth all living things were born to.

But when will that be?

And where?

Strange that I can't remember.

Final destination, port of origin … I don't even know how long I have been travelling, for what reason, under what name: my passport is a thin book of abstractions that, come to think of it, nobody ever asks to see.

The eagle is now at the far end of the concourse, strutting by the security checkpoint, a few attendants backing up slightly without any break in conversation, without so much as a turn of their heads. Its beak opens, gaping, panting against some invisible heat. It stares down at me, blinking shutter-like inner eyelids – snap snap snap – and suddenly I feel it too. Loose rocks underfoot. The smell of prickly pear. A hard, dissolving light. The burn of an outside world no air conditioner could ever subdue. With a great sweep of its magisterial wings the raptor ascends, something doomed kicking in its talons, a single huge whoosh of air, an exclamatory verdict – *I am not the apparition!* – and away it goes. Off to some distant cliff, a nest, a convocation of sleeping fledglings, an eternity of seasons. A slow-turning earth.

A cleaner moves in, sets up his small yellow sign, starts mopping and polishing away any unsightly streaks of death from polyurethane floors. He meets my stare for a moment with a sympathetic smile, shrugs, passes his hand over the top of his head in a gesture I care not to decipher. Bones and pebbles crunching underfoot, I hurry on to the next gate.

I am fox! I go wherever I go! I do whatever I do! Here in your living room, your kitchen and bathroom, right here in your bed! All night long running, leaping up your low-sheen acrylic walls and plush pile carpets – *mushroom mystique, temperate woodland beige, primrose accolade* – oh what sweet names you have for these things! What would you call this one, the gritty pigment of dew and earthen muck left as footprints all over your ceiling? *Vulpine havoc?* I am fox! I go wherever I go! I do whatever I do!

Ha ha, two-legged ape, you will never see me pass; right under your nose my whiplash trails of red flow through every crack and crevice, anointing your sacred possessions with a rank and musky odour, spattering sofa cushions with the blood of rodents you never even knew were hiding behind the skirting boards, scratching away the lice. For such fine service I help myself graciously to your fridge; I steal odd socks and keys, move bits and pieces around just to drive you crazy, an itch to the foggy complacency of your life, tiny stones in your shoes. You need these things!

Don't tell me otherwise! You who always complain about taxes and debts and rates of exchange, what do you really know of such folklore? Look at you now, all curled up in your freshly laundered bedclothes, your air conditioned nest of fibreglass and plasterboard, your four-digit codes and firewalls and top-of-the-line comprehensive cover, your cunning traps and poisons and electronic tomfoolery. None of it can keep me out! Don't you know I am as old as the blood in your veins? I was running along the wintered fibres of your soul before you were even a pup, a cub, a kit, a pulse in your mother's womb! I know your every thought and feeling, more than you do yourself, every craving, every fear and dream and vice and embarrassing secret, *I know them all*. So please, pay me no mind as I ransack the bottom drawers of your subconscious. There's nothing here that I haven't already seen a thousand times before, and a fox has no appetite for shame.

But what's this? The sun already rising! The night always so short! Quickly now, back through vents and the spaces between walls and doorframes, the magazines you will neither read nor throw out, the blinking lights of smoke alarms and answering machines; have you not noticed how red they are, just like blood and fox-fur? Quickly now, I lick off paw prints as I go, clean away excrement and remove fragments of bone. Quickly, quickly! And wait … shhh! … wait … wait … wait …

Now open your eyes and look! See how spotless everything is!

So now, here, let me help with the clocks as you rise, let me turn over each second as deftly as any claw can turn a blade of grass. Let me sharpen your razors to whisk away all unwanted fur, let me pick at invisible parasites, wrap the carrion in your fridge in clingfilm and make every toilet the mineral-blue of some imaginary Nordic lake. Let me spray every room with the fragrances you like most: *lavender morning, vanilla summer, alpine cinnamon, luscious fruit meadow* – ha, is this how you remember the forest that birthed you? So ridiculous, so endearing! Let me check that all your documents still have perfect, ninety-degree corners and fit nicely in your briefcase, that the furniture sustains correct proportions, the air is still twenty-one per cent oxygen and ... what, you think it stays like this all by itself? You'll never know how hard I work! All day long scratching away the million types of darkness and creeping rot trying to rise up and strangle this wonderful dream while you abscond to some faraway office, doing whatever it is that you do, for whatever thing it is that you believe. All will be just as you expect when you return to your big soft bed, night after night, dreaming of unremembered woodlands as we tumble together through past and future, just like always: I will never let the curtain slip! After all, dear beloved, I need you as much as you need me. And where could we live if not in the bottomless den of each other's shadow?

Where money gathers, so do pigeons. They flock to great financial centres like so many accountants in smart grey waistcoats and glittering collars, bright-eyed, strutting, nodding, darting purposefully between the fiscal-black heels of merchant bankers, bartering every waking minute for a tidy profit. A good crumb here, a good crumb there, the system always provides. They love the tall stone edifices that humans build to announce vast accumulations of power and capital. For pigeons – or rock doves as they were called many moons ago – such monuments are excellent upgrades from the seaside cliffs upon which they originally evolved. The ocean below might have been replaced by the surge and crash of invisible commodities across marble steps, but high above it all every pigeon continues to make the same sound and steady investments they always have: mates, nests, eggs, and more pigeons.

Nowhere do they do this in greater numbers than upon the grandest of all edifices, one particular stately building on the upper east side. At least, that's where it usually is. Sometimes it's on the west side, sometimes downtown, midtown, sometimes gone for days at a time. Like the pigeons themselves, it depends a lot on weather, wind direction and market forces. It just so happens that this enormous temple of granite or basalt or marble or some other expensive rock quarried from an exotic and faraway place has no fixed address. It has no *location*. For all of its elegant golden façade, it has no doors or windows. No person can live in it, no one can work in it, no one can use it or even reach it. And even if they did, there is no ground floor entry, because there's no ground floor. The building floats one thousand metres in the air, bobbing among clouds, and like all the most expensive things in the world – the wine of such rare vintage it can never be opened, the gold bullion too valuable to ever leave a guarded safe, the masterpiece too priceless to be put on public display – it's fundamentally useless.

Theories abound as to when it was built, or which architectural genius conceived of this ultimate land-grab in the air, a skyscraper to end all skyscrapers, an edifice so sublime it makes all earthbound towers seem trifling, the stuff of paltry imagination. It's not just the levitation that inspires so much awe and respect, it's the knowledge of what lies inside. From early childhood everyone is told the same bedtime story: that there is something so absolutely wonderful inside this floating treasury, so splendid it can never be seen or touched. Every coin, paper note, bond, account balance or other earthly token of value, even gold itself, is a mere symbol for this something else, safely bound within unbreakable walls, a little bit of which anyone can own, mortgage, trade, tax, borrow and grow rich upon without ever seeing. No religion could be so powerful and enduring, so binding. To see such a miracle hanging in the sky, shining down a loaded motorway as it catches the rise and fall of the sun – perfectly timed to the opening and closing hours of the stock market – is to know that all is well in the world, and that everything will always be well.

Only pigeons know the truth. They know that the building is completely empty. They found this out a long time ago, when the poorly maintained and shoddily constructed rooftop ornaments – the part which no human would ever see from the ground – crumbled under the natural duress of sun, rain and frost at such stratospheric latitudes. They began to populate it in earnest, a perfect rocky edifice filled with empty rooms that no furniture had ever touched, with no humans around to clean away their nests or bait them with poison, no rats or other vermin of the earth to bother their eggs. In short, pigeon paradise: a literal heaven in the clouds.

But being down-at-heel, street-level realists, pigeons also know that nothing good ever lasts. From high above they've seen how it goes with humans, how things rise and fall against the very laws of nature they hope to transcend. Eventually it will all go south and crash, quite literally in this case: when people stop believing in it, the pride and joy of our monetary imagination will come careening through the city like a drunken wrecking ball, taking every sacred institution with it, rendering every dollar a worthless rag, every coin a useless disc of metal, every gold bullion a good-for-nothing brick. People will desperately try to believe it back into the air, push it up with optimistic forecasts and fake projections as they've always done, but it will be too late. The image of ten million pigeons exploding from a crumbling temple packed floor to ceiling with nothing but guano is hard to erase from the mind.

But where humans are prone to panic and despair, pigeons are not. They take a much longer view. They know that this is not the end of the world, even when their bewildered human hosts have departed, leaving behind a grey wasteland of nutrient-starved concrete rubble: it is the beginning. Because somewhere, right in the middle of it all, there will have crashed the single greatest deposit of superphosphate fertilizer the world has ever seen – a fortune more real and valuable than any conceivable sum of money. From this vast basin a great forest will bloom, drawing to it all the life that had once been pushed to near-extinction by urban pretension: every plant, fungus, insect, bird, lizard and mammal, coming home to rebuild their radiant green world as rivers resume their course. Even humans may one day return to enjoy its riches, if not any of the economic lessons now concealed beneath millennial moss and lichen. Only the pigeons will ever know the truth as they scatter in search of new rookeries of hard, grey, unpollinated stone. No history of economics will ever record what pigeons already know – that they alone are humanity's greatest investment bankers.

Mr Katayama wakes in the night, puts on his boots and quietly observes himself sleeping, how the bedclothes ruck to one side and his knee sticks out the other, always the same. *I look old,* he thinks, *but peaceful. All those worries, you would never guess.* He gently wakes Mrs Katayama, who reflects upon her own body in more or less that same way. Mostly she enjoys the fact that here, standing like this at the foot of the bed, all the pain in her back and legs is completely gone. She savours the incredible sweetness of having no pain. They exchange a few comments about such things, nodding, laughing a bit. Then it's time to get the gardening tools out from under the bed and head to the stairwell.

There's always so much to do on the rooftop, you would think it was a forest they had grown up here. But no, it's just one tree. And even then not much to look at. No matter: careful pruning of the crown and the shallow roots sprawled across concrete must go on, extraction with tiny tweezers of boring worms and a host of other ravenous night bugs, then tending to various wounds and fungal infections, lesions fused by constant talking and singing. But it's always hard to tell if the tree is well or poorly, the branches are so naked, black as the night and just as shapeless.

An outsider would fairly wonder why they even bother, why not give it all up for a good night's rest? Ah, but things are as they need to be, and as long as it doesn't fall down or get completely consumed by bugs, the Katayamas attend to the tree religiously, night after night, as they've been doing now for about seventy, eighty, even a hundred years – who knows? They stopped counting many anniversaries ago.

But tonight is a different night to all the others. Tonight there is so much more to do. Tonight the tree will finally come into flower. Can you believe it? Flowers after all this time! They don't know how – they can't even see any buds – they just know it will happen. Maybe the moon is telling them, or the tree itself: time to put out all the fold-up chairs, it's saying, bust open those rusty hinges and wipe the dust off the seats.

One for their son, who will have taken two trains, four taxis and three connecting flights to get here. One for their daughter who they have not seen for so long, coming by a very different way. And then chairs for all the relatives: siblings, parents, grandparents, aunts and uncles, and all the friends and neighbours. Near or far, it doesn't matter, all distances will collapse in a moment. All of them will be here, because all of them know about the tree, and all of them have been waiting so patiently, some thousand or so letters back and forth. *Is it ready? When will it be ready? Please let us know!* Still more chairs are needed. Chairs for the barber, the grocer, the postman, the doctor, the landlord, the oncologist, the man at the department store whose name they can never remember, even for the gangly parking inspector who wrote them a ticket that one time – the day of their wedding, no less! – he was only doing his job and he had a nice enough face. Chairs for everyone they have ever met and liked, who taught them, cared for them, fought with and listened to them, even for some who merely walked by in the street or sat behind them in a restaurant, picked up a fallen spoon, or anonymously steadied their elbow on a subway step. How can they have possibly known so many people? Enough to fill a ballroom. Enough to fill a stadium. In the end they take away all the chairs; it will be standing room only.

The Katayamas discuss at length whether to put up lights, whether or not to serve drinks, canapés, play music. Should there be speeches or no speeches? An order of proceedings? They bicker and grumble and in the end they decide to do nothing much at all, they are too tired, and it is the right decision anyway. Let everyone just come for the tree, and for each other. And when they arrive, filing one by one up the stairwell and walking into the still, high darkness, let there be no fanfare. Let the greetings be hushed, whispered, because everyone can already sense some kind of pressure rising and settling along the sparse and gnarled branches of the tree. Tread quietly now, softly, as if some roosting flock of invisible feelings might otherwise take flight before anyone has a chance to look up. *Is this the tree? Oh, it's much bigger than I thought. It's so ... and you? ... oh yes ... something something...* It's getting hard to understand what people are saying as a crowd accumulates, everyone talking so low, maybe not even using real words, just participating in a collective murmur, enjoying the warmth of a strange somnambulant chant.

Oh look, here's their son! He's so big and handsome! And here's their daughter – oh, she is so small! Her happy face is round and forever bright, but there are no cries of joy or floods of tears, no painful knots in the throat this time. No need for apologies or forgiveness. Again, it's as if the tree has already caught these sentiments somewhere in its roots, ferrying them gently up to the sky, so everyone can breathe and laugh and murmur and just nod knowingly and hold hands, free of all tension. How wonderful it is to be here, yes, just like this, together in the warm dark. How wonderful to be *here*. The great grandparents, known only from photographs, look on from the lower boughs, translucent.

That murmur, it rises slowly. That's what happens when you have such a big group of people, even on rooftops like this, even when there is not much that needs saying and people are trying to keep it down. One sound raises the level for another to be heard, and this pushes back and forth, building up like an immense orchestra tuning their instruments before a show, louder and louder, enough to make you feel drunk on sound, so much so that when it suddenly stops for no apparent reason, when all mouths pause at once and turn openly to the tree, the silence that rushes in to fill the void pushes up against every throat and eardrum like cotton wool and the tree explodes into light. *Shoosh!* A million flowers! A billion! A colossal pink hemisphere rising upward so unbelievably, so massively, it's as if the whole apartment building is breathing in, like an enormous set of steel and concrete lungs, the whole architecture of existence groaning. And then, as the sheer weight of blossomy tonnage drips down like suds from an overfilling bath, drenching the night with perfume, the crowd erupts into applause.

Nobody really knows for whom they are applauding. For the tree? For such patient gardeners, the Katayamas, barely visible now beneath an avalanche of scented petals? For the simple need to pour *something* back into all that muffled bright colour: a singular joy, a wordless appreciation, a communal vibration, the sound of a hive. Yes, that's exactly what it is, the sound of a hive. Soon nobody can tell the difference between the clapping of hands and the hum of tiny wings, for here they come at last, the bees of the night, falling down from great heights like a black curtain that peels itself away from the sky and drapes gently over the entire tree, darkening, gathering as much pollen as possible within the brief moment of the blossoming. All of them buzzing like mad, too desperately busy, thank heavens, to bother stinging any of the guests. They have waited too long, life is too short, and the blossoms are already dying, unable to sustain their improbable existence. The bees zip frantically about the cascades of white and pink that bury the guests up to their waists, and even as withering blossoms are thrown back up into the night, offering the bees a final taste, all of the visitors know the moment has passed. As quickly as it came into being, the flowering is over.

The bees rise up and away to do whatever it is that bees do, and then, just like that, it's time for everyone to go home.

As for the Katayamas, they are not at all disappointed. Things have happened exactly as they need to have happened. They do not feel tired any more, but suddenly bright and lucid, light and quick, moving here and there and everywhere: so many kisses, handshakes and bows, small gifts of air and motion, laughing as they brush shrunken blossoms from the shoulders of each departing guest and tears from their own eyes. But it isn't hard to say goodbye, this time, not even to their son and daughter. Those are not tears of sadness.

When all the guests have finally left, husband and wife sit for a long time, doing nothing much at all. They just sit and breathe. Then they rise silently to shovel and rake dead blossoms over the sides of the building, watching them fall to invisible streets. It's hard, dull work, but the Katayamas find themselves enjoying this part the most. There is time to think about all the people who came, the moment of blossoming, the applause, the bees. Each knows what the other is thinking. They do not finish until it is almost dawn and the withered branches of the tree are cut down and hauled over the sides and the stump broken down with slow strikes. Thank goodness they remembered to bring an axe! On hands and knees they dust every corner of concrete, stand up to inspect, then dust again. By the time they tiptoe back down the stairwell, there is nothing left behind, nothing to see for a century of work and labour and love.

The Katayamas creep back into bed, careful not to disturb their heavy, slumbering bodies. *Just a few more minutes of rest, just a few more minutes please*, time to let things settle back into their earthly shape and mass. And when the light of morning finally glides across their fingers and faces and they rouse and shift, feeling that familiar ache in their bones, they will turn to each other and wonder, as they have done every morning since the day they first met: *Why do our mouths always taste like honey?*

Nobody knows what they are for, the things we make here. We do wonder sometimes. They are toys perhaps, or weapons. But nobody really knows. We are not paid to know.

I oversee the department where the circuit boards and switches are put in, checking that the lights and buzz-tones are all working correctly before the vitreous casings are snapped and screwed together. It's always a surprise when those casings come: that for all the fuss and work, these are nothing but vegetables. Last week it was endives. This week it's beetroots. I don't think I've ever seen a real beetroot, let alone eaten one, but I can recite the dimensional specifications of them in my sleep. I can even tell you how many soldering points, wires, brackets and diodes go in, which kind, where, and how; the swatch colour values, the net weight, product code, the heat resistance, the lithium charge, the tensile quotient. The only thing I can't tell you is what any of these things are for. Or what I would give for some *real* vegetables to take home to my family.

When I look out of the small window in the last cubicle of the upstairs bathroom and see all the office buildings receding into the fog, I think about that termite documentary I once saw on TV. How these blind ants live in super-complex colonies of mounds and tunnels, without any of them knowing what any of it is about, not even that they are underground or that they are termites. The fact that the buildings in our district are connected up with tunnels so we don't have to go outside during winter – a winter that seems to get longer every year, such that there may come a point when we don't go outside at all – well, none of that is lost on me as I wash my hands and hurry back to my station. I just heard the rumour that there are more redundancies coming, as early as next week.

Anyway, no matter how cold the winters get, we wilfully forego the tunnels and duck outside at the end of shift after the siren sounds. There is no policy. They don't seem to mind if we stand patiently by the yellow line, bracing ourselves with coats and cigarettes and umbrellas, waiting for the yak.

Ah yes, the yak, the yak. The yak is coming.

When things get hard at work and I feel like I can't stand it any more, the lifeless smell of plastic insulation, the drone of the overhead vacuum, the stuttering fluoros, the personality disorders of management, the strange sense of being *nowhere in particular*, I think of the yak. When the electric ding goes off to remind us all to look up and roll our eyeballs for a minute, check our surgical masks and back posture, give careful thought to our bladder pressure, I think about the yak. I pass my co-workers in the kitchenette during afternoon break and we all sigh, *the yak, the yak is coming*, and that murmur of consolation bypasses all the bitter aftertaste of cheap instant coffee (cutbacks) and the weary visage of our faces reflected in linoleum from a previous century. Only four more hours before the yak comes, three more hours, two, and then one. The last hour is always the easiest, even though they turn off the heating much too early; the yak is virtually here already. We don't even count the time standing out in the wind, huddled like this against the imaginary shelter of monumental pylons.

Sometimes I think I could roll back the skin on my arm and see diodes and glass, flashing lights, the order number, and I'd maybe raise an eyebrow but not much more than that, I'd just roll the skin back down and zip-lock it at the wrist. What could I do about it? As with the rest of my life, not much. Just think about mistakes. Or worse, that there have been no mistakes, that things were only ever going to be like this for all of us, no matter how hard we studied and sacrificed and dreamed. But the yak is different. In fact, it's the most real and hopeful thing I know, a shaggy old animal that management somehow forgot to sell, upgrade or retrench, and which somehow escapes the notice of everyone except us, the smallest of the company cogs. At first you can't see it against the grey, but then you focus like a monk, and it's like a soft spot that lightens, peels away from the vanishing point of the factory wall. *Oh, so slowly it moves!* But we never mind the waiting. We just huddle and listen to the bells reach our ears first, bells that are so quiet they go *under* the sound of industrial compressors where nothing could possibly rise above it.

And then in great wafty movements it's here, a wall of white hair corkscrewing all the way to the asphalt, brushing the yellow line. Small, small eyes, big snow-shovel nose, and wide horns reaching upwards as if in praise of the tin-grey sky: *hallelujah!* We grab all that white hair in handfuls like winding rope, become half buried in it as we haul our tired bodies up onto its back – so broad and soft – in each of us a final burst of strength we never knew we had. This is the best thing, the climbing up. The simple act of elevation. Sometimes I become so buried in those layered curtains of hair that I feel lost in the heartbeat of this giant furnace of an animal, and I breathe in deeply. The smell of a yak, contrary to what you might think, is deep and earthy and beautiful, strangely familiar, like something our great-grandparents might have known. The steam of its breath rolls up and over us like nourishment, like freshly baked bread or boiling noodles. Sometimes I think a yak must be the most beautiful thing in the world.

How many of us will it carry? There seems to be no measure. It just carries as many people as want to be carried: *give me your tired, your poor, your huddled masses! I will rise up and long like a mountain chain! I will take you all!* The cars, buses and trains rush past in rush-hour frenzy, but none are as pleased with their speed as those who ride the yak. It's so slow! There is time to joke and talk nonsense like children, and maybe that's what we are becoming, losing all interest in phones and newspapers, shrinking in size until our clothes become blankets, we can crawl inside our own pockets, just wanting to savour the oceanic sway of bovine hips and shoulders, this old lullaby, and feel the world shift around our ears. Sure, there's not much to see along these outskirts, but still some grace in vertical and horizontal shades of grey, speckled as they are with the red lights of traffic. It's quite pretty. You do notice such things when you ride a yak.

Many ages later we come off the flyover, migrating half-asleep to some distant and brownish part of the city untouched by sun and well below the unswept hemlines of the motorway. We release our grip on the reams of hair and allow ourselves to slide down between these shaggy shawls of bells and tassels, our bodies for a moment completely relaxed and limp until the ground rushes up to our heels and surprises us with its density. We straighten our jackets and work trousers, brush our hair. With a gentle sidestep those great woolly yak-flanks usher us forward as if blowing a paper boat across a pond, and when we walk, we drift, just like that, like paper boats, all the way across cracked footpaths and rubbish-strewn lanes and leaky stairwells, all the way to each and every bright-painted doorframe, drawn in by glowing yellow blooms of kitchen steam, children laughing and crying and clattering toys, the long lines of white crumpled linen, the chime of bells and the deep, deep, woolly smell of home. *No, I think as I take off my shoes and step inside, a yak is not the most beautiful thing in the world.*

We tell each other the same story, over and over again, just changing details here and there. We do this every time we squat in the dust splitting shale. It's such a wonderful way to pass the time. We chatter and chatter in our simian way, and the black leaves of stone fall apart so perfectly, like pages in an old book, with each tap-tap-tap of our hammers, a pleasure for which no word was ever invented. Look at the way the light floods in upon ages of darkness, raking over the grandest of all grand narratives: jellyfish, worm, frog, lizard, bird… the faint impressions of everything we once were or could have been, every gamble of nature, every birth and death. We stare at our own five-fingered hands for a moment and ponder the crazy fluke of existence: we have so many questions! But the sun bears down on our heads and burns our backs and dries up every theory and religion before it's even had time to distil. The powder-blue air stands mute as it always does. And fair enough too – our time is long past.

Still, we can't help sifting through stones, forever looking backwards. We are that kind of animal, as if the rebellion of our spines against gravity, this bizarre upright gait, had also caused some other anomaly of the eyes and mind. Always looking over our shoulder at what was. Always restlessly searching, noses too far from the ground.

And then, after all that searching, when we *do* find it, we just don't know what to think. Jammed between all the things that once walked, swam, crawled, climbed and flew, here it is, a layer-cake of rock at our knees that sparkles with granulated plastic and brittle, faintly radioactive ash. We rest our hammers, take up the small picks and brushes and set to work. We gently exhume the entangled limbs, either dishevelled by the comforts of time or locked together by the fear of it. And look, our very own skulls, side by side, almost touching, like small brown coconuts, packed full of parched loam or hollow as bells. What funny bubble-shaped things they are! Nobody will ever know the galaxies that once swirled inside them. No scientist of the future will decipher our great dreams and passions, no scientist will come at all. Some things are so completely lost, so gone, so absent, so vanished, so extinct, so … well there was never a right word for it. This is what you think about when you see yourself as a fossil.

We do wipe away tears, or possibly sweat, or possibly just the passing memory of tears and sweat – the backs of our hands come away dry – above all else it's a distant curiosity that persists. Why did we fight so much? Why were we so cruel and callous, so selfish and separate, so *lonely* on this high band of rock? Only now, too late, do we remember quietly the things that bind all brothers and sisters in sediment, each husk and bone much the same carbonate as any other: shark, bear, crocodile, owl, pig, lungfish, moonfish, parrot, pigeon, butterfly, bee, tiger, dog, frog, snail, cat, sheep, horse, yak, orca, eagle, hippopotamus, rhinoceros, fox … at least we gave them our most beautiful words.

The sun dips below the horizon and a chill nips the air, so we descend the cliff and bury all our tools under rocks. In the next valley we hear the vast murmur of every living thing that ever moved across the face of this planet, and it pours through us like rolling thunder. Oh, that song! We scale the ridge and see it, a glacial river of light moving slowly from east to west, and quickly quickly quickly we run over jagged stones to join the chorus, our naked feet as light as air.

For Helen Chamberlin

Acknowledgements

Design by Shaun Tan and Nghiem Ta
Art Photography by Matthew Stanton

Much appreciation to Sophie Byrne, Helen Chamberlin, Inari Kiuru, Julia Adams, Nghiem Ta, Ben Norland, Karen Lotz, Denise Johnstone-Burt, Frances Taffinder and the Walker Books Team; Jodie Webster, Erica Wagner, Sophie Splatt and the Allen & Unwin team; Zoos Victoria, Melbourne Museum, Paul Collins, Susan La Marca, Pam Macintyre, Stephanie Jentgens, Peter Williams, Josiah Lebowitz, Royal Melbourne Children's Hospital, Jacqui Grantford, Karen Tayleur, Lee Burgemeestre, Anna Haebich, Rosemary Stevens, Sabina Envall-Ratilainen, Tiia Viikilä, Kaisa Kastegren, Nea Orelma, Pauliina Tuukkanen, Mick Smith, Belinda Wiltshire, Emah Fox, Deans Art, Barnes, Fitzroy Stretches, my parents, Diego the parrot and Vida Kiuru-Tan.

'Crocodile' was originally published in Griffith Review 47, *Looking West*, 2015.

A version of 'Owl' was originally published in *The Hush Treasure Book*, Hush Foundation, Allen & Unwin, 2015.

'Pig' and 'Parrot' originally published as 'Papagei und Schwein' in *Was ist los vor meiner Tür?* (What is outside my front door?), edited by Stephanie Jentgens, Arbeitskreis für Jugendliteratur e.V. (AKJ), 2016.

'Butterfly' was originally published in *Where the Shoreline Used To Be*, edited by Susan La Marca and Pam Macintyre, Penguin Books Australia, 2016.

'Cat' was originally published as 'The Greatest Cat in the World' in *Rich and Rare*, edited by Paul Collins, 2015. The illustration for 'Cat' first appeared in *The Financial Times Weekend Magazine*, 2016.

'Tiger' was first published in *The Stick*, edited by Lucy Freeman and Samuel Johnson, 2017.

First published in Great Britain 2018 by Walker Studio
an imprint of Walker Books Ltd
87 Vauxhall Walk, London SE11 5HJ

4 6 8 10 9 7 5 3

This book has been typeset in Garamond

Printed in China

British Library Cataloguing in Publication Data: a catalogue
record for this book is available from the British Library

ISBN 978-1-4063-8384-3
Limited Edition: ISBN 978-1-4063-8516-8

www.walker.co.uk